MABEL HARTLEY
and the Gangster's Fortune

*Titles available in the Mabel Hartley series
(in reading order):*

Mabel Hartley and the Egyptian Vault

Mabel Hartley and the Burial Chamber

Mabel Hartley and the Crusader's Map

Mabel Hartley and the Gangster's Fortune

MABEL HARTLEY
and the Gangster's Fortune

J.E. Reddington

All rights reserved. No part of this book may be used or reproduced in any manner whatsoever without the prior written permission of the author/publisher.

All characters in this book have no existence outside the imagination of the author and have no relation to anyone bearing the same name or names. Any resemblance to individuals known or unknown to the author is purely coincidental.

First Published in Canada in 2017 by J.E. Reddington
Copyright © J.E. Reddington 2017

www.janereddington.com

Previously published in 2014 in electronic format.
ISBN 978-1-77507-00-3-0 paperback

For Toby and Lucy, my not so little darlings.

With thanks to Gray Sutherland and
Shannon Mayer for all your help and for sharing
what you know.

The Gangster's Fortune

Chapter One

One day a letter arrived, with no return address on the envelope, just my name printed in block capitals above our address: Bosun's Locker, Captain's Row, Lymington, Hampshire. I cut the envelope open with a paper knife and pulled out a single sheet of paper.

Mabel, I want to talk to you about your birth and how you wound up on the church steps. I am in Maidstone Prison. Come and see me. Mother.

Just reading those few words made me feel sick, and my head started to swim.

It was March and Hugh had stopped talking to me altogether. He was a nothing more than a shadow in my life. Only Tabby still stood by me. She was my best friend at school, and she knew intimately what my birth mother had cost me.

Grace's arrest had come as a relief for us all, but it had been a bit too easy: it seemed that she had let herself be captured. But then she'd been charged with a dozen offences, including the attempted murder of my now ex-boyfriend, Hugh.

The Gangster's Fortune

All Tabby would say was that she felt safer knowing that Grace was locked away behind bars. There were witnesses who had come forward at her trial and she'd even launched an appeal, but no one doubted she would be away for a very long time.

Hugh, however, had refused to testify against her because the idea scared him too much, or at least that was what Tabby had told me. When she showed Hugh the newspaper clipping, he protested, "What do you want me to say? My mum says I can't testify. They've got other people who've come forward. She doesn't want that lunatic to have another go at me when she gets out."

Yet I wanted to go to the prison to see her. I didn't think she could hurt me in there, but if truth be told, maybe she could, at least with her words and her story. But I wanted so much to believe she might tell me the truth that I was willing to do anything.

We were all seventeen and students at Hollingsworth School, in southern England, where we'd met three years before. Now, however, we

The Gangster's Fortune

had our futures to think of. It was 1983, and every day I was consumed with the guilt that I'd almost cost Hugh his life. It was my fault that she had stabbed him, and he'd almost bled to death. He was much more clear-headed now, but full of indifference to me.

On the weekends I spent a lot of time in my room alone, missing him and what we'd shared. I cried so much sometimes I didn't think there was a drop of liquid left in me. And then I cried some more.

I spent even more time than I cared to admit looking at photos from our dig site in Jordan the previous summer, and looking at my birth father Harris Walker, whose wanted poster I kept in my desk drawer. He had been in the helicopter in Petra, had actually thrown me in, and Hugh had managed to get me out. That was when Grace stabbed Hugh in a rage and almost killed him.

I looked around my room. It felt empty except for a few posters of New York. I'd taken down the boys from Tabby's teen magazines: there just didn't seem any point to being a teenager any more. My birth mother had taken my innocence away and now I was left with knots in my stomach and a feeling of dread that never left me. But New York still lingered on. I couldn't bring myself to abandon the dream of going to find Dutch Schultz's treasure.

The phone rang. I picked it up. It was Tabby.

"What are you doing?" she asked, as if I had all the time in the world. And of course I did, for her.

"Looking at photos of us in Jordan and trying to decide if I should visit Grace in prison." I hadn't told her about the letter yet.

"I'm sorry. Did you just say something about visiting your mental birth mother Grace in prison?"

"Yes, I did."

"So you want to be at her mercy again?"

"I want answers for what she did to Hugh, what she's done to my life, and why she abandoned me. Don't I deserve that much?"

"But, Mabel, she's mad. She's a monster. You should have nothing to do with her. And I want you to promise me you won't."

"I can't promise that, you know that, Tabby."

The Gangster's Fortune

"At least think about it, then, will you? On a lighter note, my brother Barnaby's been asking if you want to go out with him. That might take your mind off things."

"Has he?" I took a long breath. Barnaby was the sort of bloke you only thought about in your dreams. He was lovely. "And me dating your brother wouldn't upset you? I've always loved his motorcycle. Gosh, what I'd give to go out on *that*."

"I know that's the *real* reason you became my friend. And what do you mean, dating? I never said anything about dating, Mabel. I just thought you might need some cheering up with a fresh face. It might be a pleasant distraction from *you know who*. Barnaby's always asking about meeting up with you."

"What do you mean by 'always'?" I said.

"Once a week, at least."

"You're having me on, Tabby. And I'll have you know this isn't the right time for it. I'm pretty vulnerable right now."

The Gangster's Fortune

"You're not that vulnerable. In fact, I think it's high time you got un-vulnerable and started looking about."

I flopped on to my bed. There was no dissuading Tabby when she had a plan.

"You know Barnaby's lovely. I'm his sister and even I think so. You could sit down for a chat, but not here, mind you, or the crawlers (Tabby had taken to calling her parents by this pet name) would be all over you."

"They don't like me either."

"That's rot, they love you. But they are a little scared of you."

"Everyone's a little scared of me."

"So what's it going to be, Mabel?"

"Tell Barnaby I'll see him on Saturday morning and we can go down to the Marina and get a ginger beer."

"Mabel," Tabby said, "I'd come to the prison with you if you wanted me to."

"I know you would but I think it's something I have to do on my own. Besides, I don't want her to set her sights on you. Maybe Barnaby would take me up there on his motorbike," I ventured.

"I'll ask him now. Barnaby," she yelled, in typical Tabitha Mason fashion. "The crawlers aren't here so you can be on for as long as you want," I heard her say as she passed him the phone.

"Mabel," Barnaby said, coming on the phone. "I've been trying to track you down. How are you?"

His voice was so smooth, and being nineteen and all, he didn't have a care in the world, other than his bike, or so Tabby told me.

"Would you like to go out on Saturday?" I asked.

"What time can I pick you up?"

"Is ten o'clock too early? Oh, and I'll need a bike helmet."

"I'll see you at ten, then, with a helmet."

I put down the phone and jumped up and down a few times before throwing myself on to my bed and kicking my arms and legs until I got tired. I hadn't felt this happy for a very long time. I thought about lemons and making lemonade and went to get myself a glass.

The Gangster's Fortune

+++

It was ten on the dot when Barnaby arrived. I hadn't seen him since months ago at Tabby's, and when I heard the motorbike stop on the street outside our house, I rushed to the door, hoping my parents hadn't heard, and yelled out a quick, "Just going out for a while, be home soon" to them.

Barnaby was on his bike, waiting. He was wearing jeans and motorcycle boots and a black leather jacket with black gloves. He was too pretty to be in a gang, but was certainly dressed for it. He took off his helmet. His hair was long and dark and straight and hung down to about his chin. His face was chiselled and his eyes were dark brown. He smiled, showing off his beautiful teeth. Tabitha had told me he was the only child in the family not to have to put up with having braces on his teeth. Not to put too fine a point on it, he was gorgeous and there he was, coming to collect me of all people, and he *actually* looked happy about it, unlike some *other* people we know.

The Gangster's Fortune

"Ever been on a bike before, Mabel?" he said, passing me the helmet coolly.

"Not once, but I've been waiting practically my *whole* life to have a go."

"I hadn't heard that before," he said, showing me the little pins on the bike that I could rest my feet on. "You're the first one to even be remotely interested in this girl. I call her Matilda. She's a Triumph, like the one Steve McQueen rode in *The Great Escape*, which is by far the coolest film I've ever seen."

"Better than Marlon Brando in *The Wild One*?"

His eyes almost popped out of his head. "Tabby never told me you were a film buff."

"Lots of time on my hands right now," I said, coming around behind him and swinging my leg up over the saddle.

"Just to be on the safe side, Mabel, you'd better put your arms around my middle." He reached for my hands and put them on his hips. "A little tighter," he said and started the engine.

The Gangster's Fortune

You don't have to ask me twice, I thought. I wiggled around on the back seat to get comfortable and rested my head between his shoulder blades.

"Ready? Hang on tight, Mabel, I don't want to lose you on our first date. I thought we'd just ride for a while, unless there was something else you wanted to do." He put his helmet back on.

"Sounds perfect," I said, adjusting mine and trying hard not to think about riding Vespas with Hugh.

In seconds, we were away from the house. Barnaby headed straight out of Lymington, taking the bends slowly at first. It was one of those lovely spring days when you feel the sun on your skin and you think the world is waking up out of a long winter snooze.

We rode on, and it felt so good to be with him. My mind kept turning back to Hugh and I wondered if this was a betrayal, but as we hadn't really spoken for six months, that seemed a bit of a stretch. So I put it out of my mind.

Barnaby pulled in to the ferry to take us to the Isle of Wight, cut the engine, parked the bike and

The Gangster's Fortune

took his helmet off. "Fancy a trip over to the island today?" he asked.

I hadn't been to the Isle of Wight since we moved to Lymington three years before. My dad loved it there because they have pencils you can buy that are filled with sand of different colours, something the island is famous for. On the beaches you can look up at the cliffs and they're orange and red and you think that sand couldn't possibly come in that colour but it does.

When the ferry came in and let off the passengers and cars, we rode the motorcycle on and as the ramp went up, we pulled away and had our first chance to talk. We were standing on the deck, outside in the sun, watching Lymington grow smaller and smaller in the distance.

"You know I've been asking Tabby about you for years," Barnaby said, without thinking anything of it. He tucked his hair behind his ears and I wondered if he could tell I was blushing. My cheeks were burning.

"Did you know?"

"Not really," I said.

The Gangster's Fortune

"What do you think of that then?" He was so confident it was unnerving.

"It's nice," was all I could manage.

He looked at me, feigning disbelief.

"From what I remember, your girlfriends have always been taller, older and prettier."

"And you've always had Hugh. Please don't say we'll just be friends, or you don't like me that way."

"Why would I say that?"

He took an apple out of the carrier sack on the side of his bike, took a bite out of it, and then offered it to me. I took a bite too. It was juicy and the juice ran down my chin. He reached over and brushed the juice off with his hand.

"And what about that McGinley fellow?" he asked.

"Oh, that's been over since we came back from Jordan last summer. Did Tabby tell you what happened there? You've probably read about it." I sighed. "They're still digging for treasure there, based on the map we found. But you know you really shouldn't be hanging out with me. It's not safe." I put on my sunglasses.

"You don't have to hide behind them," he said.

"I'm not hiding. The sun's bright."

"So it really is over with you and Hugh then?"

"Yes," I said, glad he couldn't see my eyes.

I took another bite of the apple.

"Those are words I've been waiting to hear for a long time," he pronounced.

"Why?"

"Because you're Mabel Hartley and I never imagined I'd stand a chance with you. Come here."

He put his hand out. It was soft and warm. We stood by the railing of the ferry and he put an arm around my shoulder. I felt safe, perhaps because he was older and rode a motorcycle, and most definitely was not Hugh McGinley, and he really, genuinely, seemed to like me.

When we got to the island, we followed the traffic until we came to the turn to Tennyson Down. He stopped the bike, took his helmet off and looked back at me. "Do you feel like a walk?" Then he rubbed his hand along my hands on his chest. "It's so nice having you with me, Mabel."

I thought I might die and go to heaven.

"It's getting a bit foggy, but I think we can manage. I've brought a blanket and thought you might like to have a picnic up here with the sheep. They'll leave us alone, just curious creatures, really."

Picnics, and motorcycles! The day felt plucked from the brain of my much younger day-dreaming self. Once we parked, he took my hand and we walked up across the green fields for a good hour and the fog did roll in and then we were up at the top of the island, safe from the rest of the world.

"This seems as good a place as any to sit down, doesn't it? But it is a bit on the cold side." Barnaby took the blanket from his bag, along with a thermos, and spread it out for us. He handed me another blanket for me to get warm under.

"I need to tell you something before this gets to be more than it is now," I said.

The Gangster's Fortune

He looked up at me, and I could see he was thinking I was going to tell him this wouldn't work out.

"I got a letter from my birth mother, who's in prison. I've had absolutely nothing to do with her all my life, until last summer when she came to Petra. And now here's a letter from her. I keep it on me all the time."

I handed the letter to Barnaby. He read it and then looked at me. "And you want to go and see her? Won't that just inflame things?"

"It might, in fact I know it will, but she's the only one who's got the answers, apart from my birth father Harris, that is, and he's certainly not in prison, even though he ought to be. So she'll have to answer my questions. She's sort of trapped in there."

"Maybe that's what she wants you to think."

"Would you be kind enough to take me to see her?"

"Do I need to come in and talk to her too?"

"No, I don't want her to meet you. She's unpredictable and I wouldn't want you to be on her radar. But I'd love it if you took me. I'd feel so much safer knowing I wasn't going alone."

"Where is she?"

"In Maidstone Prison. I suppose prisoners who've been stable for the last three months are allowed to have visitors. And I'm guessing I was at the top of her list. She's a stalker, the worst kind."

"Are you scared of her?" Barnaby took his fingers and laced them through my hand under the blanket.

"That's nice," I said, liking the feel of his hand.

"Well?'

"Right. Am I scared of her? That's a bit complicated. She's my mother. But she's also a criminal and she's made it clear she wants me to join whatever activity she's involved in."

"And what makes her a criminal?"

"There are rumours I've heard. Stuff about cutting the fingers off people she doesn't like and suffocating people with mattresses. Oh, and she does embezzlement, things with money in overseas accounts. But I still don't want her to meet you or even know you exist."

Barnaby drew back. "That's quite the way to roll out the welcome mat, Mabel. What about your real parents, they're ok, aren't they? Do you want them to know about me?"

I thought about the age difference, the motorcycle, the hair, the leather and I smiled. Dad would hate it. But he didn't have as much sway in things as he used to and he knew I'd never put myself in danger that involved boys. I had enough common sense to choose the right kind of people to be around.

"You know that danger kind of follows me around, don't you, Barnaby?"

"From what I've heard you chase it down."

"What? Who told you that?" I asked sarcastically.

"Who do you think?"

"Tabby."

"Of course it was Tabby. She's been so worried about you."

The Gangster's Fortune

"I know. But with Grace away, this might be our chance to go to America for the summer and see my roommate from Petra, Jules. She's great. You'll love her."

Actually, she was the sort of girl all boys loved. Beautiful, a touch bohemian, and very leggy, in fact she loved nothing more than showing off her skin. I wondered if I'd get to introduce her to Barnaby.

In my head I could hear her voice, "So this is the new Hugh. Nicely done, Mabel."

"You think your parents would let you go to America?" he asked, and I wondered if I was already in love. I tried not to look at him.

"I've been saving up, working in my dad's office. You know he's a policeman, don't you?"

"Kind of hard to miss. He pulled me over once for a broken tail light. I don't think he liked the look of me."

"He doesn't like the look of anyone male."

"Oh, I see."

"Just a touch overprotective. So will you take me to Maidstone?"

The Gangster's Fortune

"Weren't there some riots there recently, after a clampdown on prison privileges?"

"There were, probably led by my mum. She's a bit of an instigator too."

"So how did they catch her? Tabby said they'd been trying for years."

"Dad said they circled the net and drew her in. Mostly by tailing her and doing stakeouts where they followed her every move. She stayed in one place too long and they went in. It was over a car mechanic's shop, and Dad says she wasn't even surprised, didn't even try to run. She just said, 'At last.'"

"So she wanted to be caught then?" Barnaby had rolled on to his side and was picking daisies out of the grass. I looked at him. "You don't look like a daisy chain kind of man," I said.

"I don't look like a lot of things, Mabel. But I'll take you to Maidstone, if that would give you some peace, because I can see that's what you need right now and I'm happy to keep you company. More than happy. Now, won't you have something here? I got some sandwiches, I made them, not my mum, and some chocolate and cheese and crisps."

"Thanks, Barnaby," I said. "This is something else."

"I was hoping you'd say that. I'm no artist, but I do like to be out in the open. I do like you, Mabel, even though I can't really see your eyes when you've got that trucker hat on. Take it off, would you?"

I took it off and lay it on the blanket and picked some crisps out of the bag. My hair must look a sight, I thought. I pulled off the elastic band holding it back. I'd kept it a honey blonde colour and it reached down to my chest. The curls were softer now, and with a little mascara and light lipstick, I felt pretty. I was still the smallest girl in my form, and I knew I couldn't ever hope to be more than five feet tall, but that didn't seem to matter so much anymore. I had a leather jacket too - I'd found it in a thrift shop - and jeans and a Duran Duran t-shirt I'd cut the arms off of. I closed my eyes and lay back on the blanket. I didn't want to leave.

"You all right?" Barnaby said.

The Gangster's Fortune

"I haven't felt this good for a long time. It's just so easy being with you. Tabby was right, you are perfect for me."

"She didn't actually say that, did she?"

He slid over beside me and I lay down with my head on his chest. He put an arm around my shoulder and I closed my eyes again, thinking about New York City in the summer and how I was ever going to convince my parents to let me go.

Chapter Two

It took me a few weeks to get up the nerve to write back to Grace in prison. And when I finally did, it was to arrange a visit. I wanted answers that only she could give me. Barnaby had promised not to tell a living soul about driving up to Maidstone and when Grace wrote back it was to say that I could come whenever I liked during visiting hours, which were between eleven and twelve o'clock every day.

Barnaby and I decided to go on a Saturday. I had introduced him to my parents and it had all been very awkward. He'd come in the door, with his motorbike parked outside, which was not lost on my dad, and then he'd been invited for a cup of tea.

"I'd prefer coffee if you have it," Barnaby had said, taking off his jacket. I put it on the bottom of the banister, but not before I'd thought about lifting it up to my nose so I could catch a whiff of his cologne, which was intoxicating.

The Gangster's Fortune

"Come through here, to the kitchen," my dad said, leading us down the hall from the front door. Dad's office was on the right and as he passed it he pulled the door closed. He was not in uniform and that was a good thing because when he is he can be quite intimidating. But Barnaby, as I was getting to know, wasn't intimidated by very much.

"Ever been to prison?" my dad half joked, but I could tell he wasn't joking, not really.

"No," Barnaby said, "just a few tickets for speeding. Nothing to worry about."

"That's right, I remember seeing you." We were in the kitchen now. It was sunny and bright yellow, with lots of light streaming in through the windows. The kitchen table was round and wooden, with a massive jug of daffodils in the middle. "I'll just get these out of the way," Dad said, moving the flowers off to the side counter, and we sat down.

"Now, where were we?" He stared intently at Barnaby. "You don't look a thing like your sister, lad, but you are her brother? That's in your favour, particularly with Mabel. What does she think of the two of you spending time together?"

The Gangster's Fortune

"Dad!" I said getting the coffee from the cupboard. There was no reason I shouldn't have one too.

"Not having tea, Mabel?" Mum asked joining us in the kitchen. She kept her hair long and straight, almost jet black now, and her complexion was fair. She was a beauty and every day she was at home Dad told her that.

She'd spent a month having the kitchen redone, and it was just getting put back together. She had been saving from all her jobs flying around the world as an airline stewardess and had told Dad he couldn't begrudge her a few new appliances and an apron sink. My mum had a real a flair for interior design and I'd even encouraged her to go back to school for it. That way she wouldn't be away so much, but with only one year left for me at Hollingsworth it didn't really matter if she was or not.

I would be gone soon too, probably off to uni, just coming home for the holidays. I'd be on my way to a life of my own, completely independent, which was pointing more and more in the direction of a job with MI5, the spy and counter-intelligence agency that is responsible for ensuring the country's security. I wanted to be part of it, stopping people like my birth mother Grace, and having the authority to do so seemed the only meaningful thing to me. But you didn't just apply for a job with MI5. You had to be *selected* and that usually happened after you had got at least one degree. I picked up the thread of the conversation again.

"Yes, Barnaby," my dad went on, "Mabel said you and Tabby get along quite well. It must be nice to have a younger sister."

"She's a real force," Barnaby replied. He was sitting at the table with his legs spread wide apart, leaning back on his chair with his arm on the back of mine. I could tell he was making my dad nervous.

I would bet anything Dad was wishing Hugh would come back. But to his credit, Barnaby was polite and said how grateful he was to Tabby for introducing us, as he'd heard I wasn't the kind of girl Tabby was used to meeting at Hollingsworth.

The Gangster's Fortune

"That's a bit of an understatement," my dad coughed into his hand. "Do you know what they get up to, my boy?"

"Yes, Tabby showed me all the newspaper clippings. They've been very lucky, but Tabby says it's not really luck, it's more that Mabel has a nose for treasure and she might be off to visit her friend in New York now that her birth mother's in prison at Maidstone."

"It's a possibility, isn't it?" Dad looked over at Mum, who was biting her lip.

"We hate it when she's away," Mum said.

"That's a load of rubbish," I butted in. "You're the one who's always away, Mum."

Barnaby laughed and then stifled it with his hand.

"But I'm not seventeen and an intrepid person who likes getting into trouble, am I?" Mum said.

I wanted to add that she didn't have a birth mum who was in prison either, but I knew better than to come out with that. Neither of them would approve of my visit to Grace and I wasn't going to tell them until after we'd been and gone.

I felt I had a right to get the answers from her, to find out what nobody else could tell me. They hadn't told me the truth, my mum and dad, that I had been adopted, for more years than I cared to remember, so I felt completely justified, and with Barnaby to help me get there, it felt as if it was something a grown-up version of myself might do. I liked the Mabel who had finished school and was away from the heartbreak of seeing Hugh every day. I often wished he'd taken his mum up on her offer to go to another school somewhere else up north just so he could get away from me. Just seeing him hurt me so much, and even though I'd found out how to push the pain down, it always bubbled back up again. I had given him up but I had not forgotten him.

"Mabel," my dad said, looking irritated.

"Yes, Dad?"

He sounded very formal. He was going grey early and getting thick around the middle and said he had to stop being behind a desk. He missed going out on calls and tried to get to the gym a few times a week but it didn't seem to stop the spread.

"About New York. Have you heard from Jules? Do you think her mother would be all right with having you come?"

"I've just written to her and she said we could come after the end of term in June. Barnaby wants to come too, don't you?"

Barnaby looked at his lap for a second and rubbed his lip before looking up at my father, who had a very disagreeable look on his face.

"I thought it sounded like fun, but nothing's been arranged yet. And with Mabel's mother in prison there's no real danger, is there?"

"You'd be surprised," Dad said. "Harris is still on the loose. He's been a problem before. There's no reason to think he's dropped off and gone on an extended holiday in Greece. I think he must still be fronting Grace's operations but we don't know more than that."

"There is no danger now, is there love?" Mum said, more to Dad than anyone else.

The Gangster's Fortune

"It's naïve to think he's not prowling around, doing her bidding," Dad said, and a shudder went up my spine.

"I still can't believe she's behind bars. It was as if she just walked into it. Just waited there for your dad to come and get her, after Petra, you know they were in Jordan, don't you Barnaby?" Mum said.

Things were hard between us. We always seemed to be at cross purposes. And thinking back on it, it was after I found out I'd been adopted. That felt like a betrayal, something they'd held back from telling me, and it was taking me a long time to rebuild the trust between us.

"Yes," Barnaby said, "Tabby sent us the letters and then of course I saw it all over the news."

"It was the strangest thing," Mum murmured under her breath. "She did everything she could to hurt them, to take Mabel away, and none of us were prepared for it, and then she just let herself get arrested."

The Gangster's Fortune

"A woman with her kinds of connections doesn't just let anything happen." Dad said. "We did the work to find her, don't take that away from us, love, there were stakeouts and phone taps and…."

"Just like she did to us. But I can't help but wonder," Mum said, "why she gave up."

"I wasn't going to tell you, but I can't help it," I said, "so here it is. Grace has written to me and Barnaby and I are going to see her. Well, Barnaby isn't, but he's driving me."

"On his motorcycle?" Dad moved his chair away from the table, taking his cup and moving to the sink. "Why on earth would you do something like that, Mabel? Frankly, it's irresponsible to even think of doing such a thing. I thought more of you, Barnaby."

I hated it when my dad said things like that.

"You know nothing, young man, coming here with all this talk of going to see a vigilante, and might I mention that the last fellow who tried to help Mabel almost died in Jordan, and if the knife had been half an inch closer to his heart, he would have come back in a coffin."

The Gangster's Fortune

"I know what happened to Hugh," Barnaby said, standing up and putting his hands on the table, "but I'm not Hugh and the woman's in prison and Tabby's told me everything about Mabel in the last few years, everything."

"Everything?" I asked wondering what that meant.

"Just how brave you are and how much of a fighter you are and how you've discovered all these wonderful treasures, and you've never been in it for anything except to rediscover them, and how somehow you are the most fabulous person that any bloke would be lucky enough to know. What I can't understand is how Hugh could walk away from you. But that's his business and my opportunity." His cheeks flushed.

"Well," Dad said, running water into his teacup to rinse it. "Good to hear you're so well informed. But about New York, and frankly about going to Maidstone, I'll not have it. You're to stay right here, my girl. Your adventures are at an end, so you'll have to find another girl to piggy-back some excitement off, Barnaby. Our girl's not on the market."

"Please stop talking about me as if I was only thirteen. I'm almost a grown-up and I'll go and see my birth mother because I want answers from her, and you telling us we can't go isn't going to change *a thing*. I told you because I thought you deserved to know, something you never did for me until you were forced to."

Dad winced.

"I never should have mentioned it. Barnaby and I are going tomorrow. And if you try and stop me you'll have more than a trip to a prison to worry about. You'll be worrying about me not living under your roof."

"That's enough of that madness," my dad said, and then he turned to Barnaby. "You seem like a good man, Barnaby, but please, keep away from my daughter. You're too old for her and we can't have you getting hurt. I already have the guilt of one boy's near-death on my hands, so please don't make it two."

The Gangster's Fortune

"Barnaby," I said, "I am so sorry for this. It's not normal. Nothing's normal about me. Mum and Dad, I was trying to be honest, which is more than what you've been with me for most of my life. So if you don't want to lose me, I suggest you let me go and find the answers you were never able to give me."

+++

Barnaby picked me up at eight the next morning. It was a beautiful April day, and I feared that he was going to come and tell me it was off. I heard the bike and then Mum rushed down the stairs.

"I wanted to catch you before you left. Don't tell her anything about yourself, Mabel. Don't let her into your heart."

"I wasn't planning on it," I said, grateful we were still on speaking terms. "I just need to know why she left me on the church steps. I need to know that, Mum, it's eating me alive, and I need to know why she came back and what she thinks I might be able to do for her. She said she wanted me to join the business. I need to tell her to leave me alone."

"We support you." My dad stepped out of the study. "But be safe. And leave her behind for good. That's all we want for you."

"I love you both," I said hugging them.

"What about Tabby?" Mum said.

"I'll call her tonight when I get back."

Barnaby knocked at the door. I opened it.

"Ready?"

He saw my parents standing behind me. "I'll look after her, not a scratch, I promise."

My mum turned and ran back up the stairs and my dad went into his office without saying a word.

We shut the door behind us, and walked over to the motorcycle. I hopped on the back behind him.

"Right then. Maidstone, here we come," he said as we put on our helmets

+++

The Gangster's Fortune

It took us two hours to reach the prison and when I got off the bike my bum was numb and I had pins and needles in my legs.

"Are you sure you still want to do this?" Barnaby asked taking my hand, once we'd taken off our helmets.

"I'm not sure now that we're here. I can't believe she's really in there. It's so surreal. It feels like, well, not how I thought it would. The last time I saw her, she was so menacing. Just frightful and I don't know what I'll say now I'm here."

"It'll be over before you know it and you'll be glad you came, at least I hope you will. And you know that if she says things that upset you, Mabel, you can always leave, but she can't."

We went inside and met a clerk who asked for my name and date of birth, and I handed her my Visiting Order, which Grace had sent. Barnaby said he'd wait for me there. I told her Grace's first name because I simply didn't know what her surname might be, and the clerk gave me a look that seemed to say I was too young to be visiting people in prison.

"She's my mother," I managed to get out.

"I'd rather you than me," said the female guard, who had huge black boots on. Her hair was slicked back into a ponytail and her eyes were stone cold.

"I shan't be long," I said to Barnaby.

"Take as long as you need, I brought something with me to read." He reached into his jacket pocket and pulled out a paperback.

The guard opened the gate and let me inside, and then took me through to a room with a row of chairs in it, each one in its own cubicle, with a glass partition. On the other side of the glass there was another chair and a phone attached to the wall.

"She could be out in five years," the guard said, "but I expect you know that, good behaviour, and all."

She gestured for me to sit down. I looked across at the empty chair and wondered if Grace would come in. I couldn't believe I was here and this was where we were meeting. I had the feeling that she'd planned it all.

I'd dreamt about this moment and the dreams had always turned into nightmares. And then, there she was in front of me. My mother. She was wearing a uniform with grey and black horizontal stripes. She smiled and sat down, picking up the phone on her side of the wall and I did the same.

I wasn't sure I could say a word. I wanted her to apologize for stabbing Hugh, for almost killing him, for leaving me when I was just an infant, and for being so evil. But these weren't things I thought she'd ever be sorry for.

"Mabel, I've been waiting for you for so long," she said, and I could see that it wasn't difficult for her to be in prison. She leaned forward and for a second I wondered if she was going to try to put her fist through the glass. "It's so kind of you to come. I knew you would if I was locked up." She so sounded normal. She looked normal. Her hair was like mine, and I guessed she was about thirty-five years old. But her smile was icy and she looked vengeful.

"What do you want with me?" I said.

"To be your mother, of course."

"It's a bit late for that, don't you think?"

"It'll never be too late. We're of the same blood. They've just been keeping you for me until I was right in the head. But the real question, Mabel, is why are *you* here?"

"To get answers."

"I knew you'd come if I was inside." She smiled smugly. "That's how much I wanted to meet you. Under different circumstances than last time. So I let myself get caught. Didn't you want to meet your mummy?"

"You're not my mother, not really," I said, and her eyes seemed to grow even darker. "So why did you leave me? Why did you stab Hugh? I loved him, you know."

"But not anymore? You see, this is how this is going to work, Mabel. You're going to tell me something about yourself and I'll tell you something you want to know. Those are my terms."

"What do you want to know?" I asked her.

"What happened with Hugh?"

The Gangster's Fortune

"He left me. We don't talk any more. I miss him. But you did that. You scared his mother stiff and now he hates me."

"That's a bit of strong word, isn't it? I'd bet he doesn't hate you."

"Well, it's your fault if he does."

"You be nice, Mabel."

"Why did you leave me on the church steps?"

"I didn't."

"What do you mean you didn't?"

"Someone else did."

"You mean my father, Harris?" I asked.

"No, someone else took you away from me. I wanted you, Mabel. I wanted my little girl and but then someone stole you from me."

"Who?"

"That's a new question. Play by the rules, Mabel."

"But I don't understand. If you wanted me how could you let someone else steal me?"

"I was a young girl then, just like you. It seems such a long time ago now. Harris and I wanted to keep you. But we knew we had to hide you." Her eyes watered for a second.

"What do you mean, hide me?" I was starting to feel something like panic.

"We couldn't tell anyone about it, about the baby, about you. So I hid you. Because I knew if he knew then I'd never be able to keep you. And I wanted so badly to be your mother. I wanted us to be together, just as I do today. And I know you want the same. Tell me Mabel, how are your plans to go visit New York? Are you still going this summer?"

"How do you know about New York?"

"I know things, Mabel. I may be inside but it doesn't mean I still don't hear things. You can understand that. And you ought to go, Mabel, maybe you should even take that new boy of yours with you. Barnaby? That's his name, isn't it? Makes me suspect you really didn't love Hugh after all, did you?"

"You keep away from them."

"What could I do in here?" Grace smiled.

The Gangster's Fortune

"Sorry, I need to go now." I felt as if I was going to be sick.

"You can come back any time, Mabel. A mother loves seeing her daughter, even under these awful conditions. I hope you got what you came for. I certainly did."

She hung up the phone and stood up but before she walked away, she put her hand on the glass. There was a note in her palm. I could only just make out the writing.

I will take you back.

"Please let me out." I ran over to the guard, who quickly ushered me out of the room and led me to the gate. She unlocked it for me and I rushed out to where Barnaby was sitting.

"You all right?" he asked, standing up and smoothing my hair.

"Let's get out, away from here, away from her."

"Did you talk to her?"

I nodded.

The Gangster's Fortune

"She put her hand up on the glass partition. It had a note on it saying she's going to take me back."

"Take you back? Where?"

"I don't know. Take me back, as if I belonged to her, was her property."

"But she's in prison. How's she going to do anything from in there?"

I shook my head. "I don't know."

"Did she say anything else about why she left you?"

"She said she didn't leave me; someone else did."

"Who?"

"Someone she had to hide me from."

Barnaby looked at me and pulled me in close to his chest. "Well at least you got something out of this. That's good. Right?"

"I think I just stoked the fire. My parents were right. I never should have come. Can you take me home with you? I can't face my parents right now. I think I need to talk to Tabby."

The Gangster's Fortune

Chapter Three

"What do you mean, you both just came back from the prison?"

Barnaby was putting his key in the lock when Tabby opened the door, demanding to know where we'd been.

"You weren't visiting your mother, were you? Yes, yes, you were," Tabby's eyes grew huge. "What was it like?"

"It was built out of stone, and very old, hundreds of years old, with a huge wooden door. It looked more like a convent than a prison," Barnaby said, "but this is England, everything looks thousands of years old here. They never build anything new, at least not around these parts."

"But I don't believe it. You promised never to see her again and here you are trotting off with him!" She glared at her brother, who shrugged his shoulders.

"The crawlers are out on a showing, and they won't be back for hours. We can go to the kitchen.

The Gangster's Fortune

That's us, Barnaby, not you, so why don't you go and polish your bike and practise looking nice for Mabel. I knew this would happen again. Didn't I tell you, Barnaby, how left out I used to feel with Mabel and Hugh? And now you've come along and taken Hugh's place and here I am all left out all over again." She pouted.

"Pardon me," Barnaby objected. "I haven't taken anyone's place."

"Yes, yes, you're right, I'm sorry, but really, going to the prison and then showing up here afterwards, what do you both expect me to do? It's like something out of a play by Shakespeare and now I'm about to get stabbed by a villain who's hiding behind the curtains. That was *Hamlet* I think, or was it *Macbeth*? Lots of knifing in both, really."

I stared at her.

"Poor choice of words," she went on. "Sorry. Oh, I can't stop saying that. Someone save me from myself and tell me what happened before I make a complete dog's mess of everything. I mean, I'm so jealous I could almost spit, and I can't believe you picked Barnaby over me for something as important as this, but I suppose I can't drive on my own yet. They never should have failed me on my learner's test, and there really isn't enough room for the three of us on the bike, and do your parents know where you went today?" She prattled on and on.

I nodded.

"Isn't that something! And they let you go?"

Tabby had grown up to about six feet tall now and looked something like an Amazon. She'd also taken up rugby and was the strongest player on her team, purely for her strength and agility, which she attributed to her years in karate, which she also did to keep fit. It was Tabby's passion and she was convinced, now that she'd grown out of her baby fat, that the boys would be queuing up to watch her playing rugger. They couldn't miss her. She was the only girl with ginger hair and a long thick plait going down her back, and freckles absolutely everywhere.

I'd been to one or two of her rugger matches and had only seen Hugh there. She said they were still talking to each other, but I supposed that meant only when I was nowhere near. So I stopped going because he'd only look over at me and nod. Never a wink, never a smile, or the slightest move to come over and join me. Nothing. It was hopeless. He was hopeless, not devoted to me in the slightest. But he'd show up for Tabby's rugger matches, and I hated him for that, and I'd even asked her if she liked him and to promise that she'd never, ever go out with him. To which she'd replied, "Don't worry, he's not my type."

I didn't believe her. Boys were her type.

I looked at Barnaby with his back to us in the fridge, making a sandwich, with his broad shoulders and long torso.

"The prison was quite nice, actually," he said, taking things out of the fridge and putting them on the counter. "Nothing like what you'd see in the films, looked more like a school."

"Must you go on?" Tabby glared at him.

"Mabel went in. I just gave her a lift."

"You were a lot more than that," I said.

The Gangster's Fortune

"Oh, really," Tabby said, "I go off on one rugby tournament and suddenly you two are in love."

I felt myself blush. It was becoming a habit with these two.

"We're not in love, yet," Barnaby said, looking at me and then narrowing his eyes. "Are we?"

I couldn't help but laugh. Tabby laughed too. And then we were all laughing and Barnaby was asking who else wanted a sandwich. We ate with some fizzy drinks around the island in the kitchen. Tabby's two other brothers had left home, and Barnaby was the only one left with Tabby.

"Didn't you have to go to work today, Barnaby?" Tabby asked.

Barnaby had a job at the local newspaper. He wanted to be a journalist and was getting experience.

"I took the day off," Barnaby said. "Well, it was important. Mabel needed me."

"So it is love," Tabby said. "I'll tell you I won't be left out again. We'll have to have some ground rules if you're going to be around us."

The Gangster's Fortune

"I'm your brother, Tabby," Barnaby said, staring at her so intently that it looked as if he wanted her to leave off. "You love me, really you do and I'm a good sort, one of the best, or you wouldn't even have let me have a word with Mabel here."

"I needed to do something to mend her broken heart, didn't I? But it might be working a little too well. So, how was she? Did you see her? Was she mad? Are you going to go back?"

"I can't face her again. It was like looking at a twisted, awful, conniving version of me. She looks so normal on the outside but inside her heart is black."

"How can you tell that?"

"She did stab Hugh."

"Yes, there's that," Tabby said, taking a sip of her fizzy drink. "But maybe she's becoming a better person."

"I don't think so. She put a note up to the glass saying she'd take me back."

"By force? By mind spells? What did she mean?" Tabby looked worried.

The Gangster's Fortune

"I think she meant to scare Mabel," Barnaby said. "And it worked."

"But she is in prison. We can't forget that. She's behind bars, probably sleeps in a padded cell. I wonder what she's up to in there."

"That's what we'd all like to know. But somehow, she's also found out about Barnaby and New York," I said, suddenly losing my appetite and offering my sandwich to Tabby.

"New York, but how? We're not even going, are we?"

"We might be," Barnaby said.

"We? Does that mean you think you're coming too?" Tabby said. She looked at me.

"If Barnaby wants to come, why not?" We hadn't talked about it yet, but I'd wanted to bring it up.

"Back at the beginning," Tabby taunted her brother, "if you wanted to go looking for long-lost treasure you had to be at Hollingsworth."

"But we're not at the beginning any more are we, Tabby? Grace has seen to that. And if Barnaby wants to come, then I'd say we couldn't have better company."

"Company for what?"

We heard a door slam. Tabby's parents came into the kitchen.

"New York City," Tabby started to singing an old Frank Sinatra song about New York and Barnaby put his hands to his ears.

"Another trip with Mabel?" Their mum said. I couldn't tell if she was for or against. "But your birth mother's in prison now, isn't she? So it's quite safe." The way she said it, it sounded more like a question.

"Quite safe, in fact they went to visit her today," Tabby stopped and stared at me. "Sorry," she mouthed. Tabby had a bad habit of not having a filter on anything she was saying at any time. And sometimes it was too much.

"Anyway, it all went fine, and they bonded and she's quite all right now, isn't she Mabel? It's as if she's having a rebirth or something, given up being a baddie."

The Gangster's Fortune

Tabby's father stared at her and then at Barnaby. "Was that good judgement, son?"

What was she talking about? I closed my eyes and sighed. Why was this my life?

"It's all fine, Dad, and it's so fine that the girls and I were talking about going to New York this summer."

"What's the treasure you're looking for this time?" their father asked, looking genuinely curious but a little alarmed. He'd cut his red mutton chop sideburns so they were a little closer to where his ears started on his head. I had always been fond of him. He wanted so much for Tabby to like him, but she never noticed. All she'd say was that he was *so boring*. Never to his face of course but still, he knew, or why on earth would she want to be friends with me? Tabby liked adventure as much as I did. She just didn't always have the stomach for it.

"It's a gangster's fortune," I said, "someone called Dutch Schultz, who was a crook in New York back in the 1930s. He buried some treasure somewhere in the New York area and we, well - Tabby and I - we were thinking about going over to see our friend Jules, and also seeing if we could find it."

"America is such a long way away," Tabby's mother looked a little scared. "But I suppose we can't stop you and if the lunatic's in prison it ought to be quite safe, shouldn't it? And Tabby, you said Jules lives in Manhattan, that's quite a safe place I believe. It might be nice to get out of England and go on another adventure... now that there's no threat to your safety."

Tabby's mother had struggled with depression and it wasn't like her to support anything we'd dreamt up. But she was wearing brighter colours now, and I noticed she had rouge on her cheeks, new shoes on, and a proper, smart briefcase. Not that saying someone who is depressed can be snapped out of it by getting a new handbag, but it certainly goes a long way when that someone is out leading a normal life again and, on this day, supporting us.

"And with Barnaby with you, you'd be quite safe, if you wanted to go, dear. It might be your last chance before you have to get serious at uni, and

The Gangster's Fortune

weren't you were saying you might write something about the adventure for publication?"

For the first time I looked at Barnaby and I could see he was having trouble finding the words.

"Is that the only reason you wanted to come? To have a story to write? Because if that's all it is to you, well, I should go," I said bluntly, feeling disappointed and angry.

"Did I say something to put you out of favour, Barn?" his mum said, and then I heard her say, "I'm sorry, dear." I wondered if she meant it.

I hurried over to the door to get my coat, and he was at my heels.

"Mabel, wait, I just said that so they'd consider letting me go, so they wouldn't think I just wanted to go because I like you. I had to make it sound proper."

"A little too proper for my taste."

He ran his fingers through his hair and put his hand on the back of his neck. Then something happened and I leant in and kissed him. He looked as surprised as I was. It was lovely.

The Gangster's Fortune

"I'd love you to come, Barnaby. I love the idea that you want to come and if you write a splendid story about it, well, so much the better."

I surprised even myself but I was tired of feeling wretched. So what if he wanted to write a story about going to New York? It didn't mean he didn't have real feelings for me. I told myself to stop thinking the worst about people who cared for me.

We turned around and there were Tabby and her parents, all looking on from the kitchen.

"Right, then, Mabel," Barnaby coughed and turned away from his family. "Could we do that again, somewhere else?" he whispered.

"I'll think about it," I said, smiling and patting his chest with my hand. "But could you give me a lift home now?"

"We'll take you, won't we?" Tabby piped up. "Barnaby can drive Dad's car. You can't leave me out of everything."

"Take Mum's car instead, I don't want mine dinged up. You're a fine driver, son, but in a fit of excitement…" he trailed off.

"Dad, would you give me the keys, please."

The Gangster's Fortune

The three of us walked down the path between the stone lions.

"I like to rub their heads for good luck," Tabby said, patting the lion in front of her. "It works, you know. My mum's quite keen about letting us all go to New York. That's a bit of luck, isn't it? It sometimes feels like she's had a lobotomy. But of course she hasn't, has she, Barn?"

"Don't be ridiculous," he said, opening the car door for me. "I think we'd know if she had, it's a big operation, isn't it?"

I giggled to myself, getting in.

"I suppose I'm in the back then," Tabby said. "You could be the driver and we could both be in the back, Mabel."

"That's not exactly fair to Barnaby, I'd prefer to sit in the front."

"Suit yourselves," she got in and put on her seatbelt, crossing her arms in front of her chest. "Nothing like being a third wheel *again*," she muttered under her breath.

+++

The Gangster's Fortune

At school the next week, all Tabby and I could talk about was writing to Jules and seeing about dates. We thought we might go for a month in the summer but we needed to ask about Barnaby coming too. We were chattering away, when someone put a tray down beside us. Thinking it was Sam, who was in our dormitory every year, and sometimes joined us, I didn't bother looking up.

"Sam," I said, "we're planning on taking a trip to New York this summer."

"So I hear."

I looked over and Hugh was beside me, at my elbow. "Tabby said her parents and yours had given you the go-ahead and you visited your mum in prison and that there's no getting her out of there. Is that true, Mabel? Are you really going to go and see Jules?"

Hugh was taller now and still towered over me as he always had. How did I find these Amazon people for friends? He looked sad, and a bit pale, and something seemed to have gone out of his eyes. But irritatingly so, he was handsome as ever and totally crushing his loneliness. I wanted to slip my hand into his, but I kept it firmly clenched around my fork. The blonde hair, the blue eyes, the long whiskers, those ruddy cheeks. I hated him for looking so smart in his uniform and for never, ever looking the worse for wear.

"Barnaby might be going with us," Tabby jumped in.

"Who's Barnaby?" Hugh asked.

"Only my brother! He and Mabel are a bit of a thing now, though neither of them will admit it, and he's probably coming, at least we'd like him to. Did I forget to mention that bit about the trip?" Tabby said and I could tell she was relishing the fact.

"Yes, you did leave that bit out and I can see why. Well, good for you. Be nice to have someone else around so it's not just you girls, if you get into trouble, which you will of course, won't you?"

"Why are you even here sitting with us, Hugh?" Tabby was never one to mince words. "You've been avoiding Mabel like the plague all year. Don't think I'm the only one that's noticed."

"I suppose I couldn't stay away," he looked at the other tables. I wondered if he cared that people were staring at us.

Everyone knew we had been together and everyone knew that Hugh wasn't allowed to speak to me. I was surprised that someone hadn't intervened on his mother's behalf just as he sat down. I looked about but no one was rushing over to rescue him from me.

"But you've managed to since Jordan. And I can understand that," I pushed the mashed potato around my plate. "But that said, what's changed for you? Is our mother suddenly the biggest member of my fan club? That would be a switch, wouldn't it?"

"She was just trying to keep me safe, that's why I didn't testify." He looked defensive.

"No one expected you to testify, Hugh," I said. "The last thing we need is to have you hurt again. She did enough damage in Jordan to last us a lifetime, that much is clear."

"But I want to hear about the trip. I want to come too, I suppose."

The Gangster's Fortune

"Well, I never," Tabby said, "crawling back with your tail between your legs when you think there might be an adventure on the way. It's pathetic."

"Tabby, he did come to your rugby matches. He's been a good friend to you."

"I was just trying to be supportive, Mabel. You don't want him to come with us, do you?" She looked flabbergasted.

Hugh looked at me and I felt my tummy turn to jelly. We hadn't made eye contact in months. He put his hand on mine and squeezed it gently. My breath caught in my chest.

"I haven't forgotten about all the fun we had in Scotland, you know, or in Jordan, before the helicopter, and most of all I haven't for a second forgotten how I used to feel when we were together, Mabel, even though you have, and even though you've found someone new, I have never stopped caring about you and wanting the best for you."

The Gangster's Fortune

I was a terrible, terrible person who didn't deserve to even sit next to someone like Hugh. That was what I thought about myself just then.

"And now your mum's in prison, well my mum's begged off a bit, and she asked if you'd come for tea and brighten things up a bit for me. She knows how miserable I've been but I couldn't stand the idea of being sent away from you."

I felt my eyes water and my chin started to tremble.

"Hugh McGinley, you should be an actor. What a load of rot," Tabby said.

"It's not rot, it's not. I thought it might be an idea to come and sit with you but now I can see I'm not welcome. So I'll be off."

"Hugh," I said. "It's good to talk to you. The best really. I'm glad you're doing better and things are easier with your mum. I never meant for anything bad to happen to you. I'm so sorry that it did. I suppose I just never knew how life would be without you. How empty it would be. But things are changing now, you can understand that. And we don't know about my birth father Harris, where he is, or if he might follow us to New York and do something dreadful, and it's just better if you're not involved this time."

"Because of Barnaby?"

"Yes, also because of Barnaby, but I don't want you to get hurt again and you never know what might happen. It usually ends badly and I won't have you almost getting killed again. You can understand that, can't you?"

"It'll be better if I'm not there, that's what you're really trying to tell me, isn't it, Mabel?" He got up, picked up his tray, turned on his heel and left.

I turned back to Tabby, whose jaw was on the floor.

"Mabel Hartley," she said, as if announcing it to the room. "You've been waiting for him to come back, pining for him, and now you're sending him away?"

"But what about Barnaby? I can't, I mean I don't know what's the right thing to do. Barnaby wants to come, he wants to be with me. And what about Harris? We've never even talked about that, have we Tabby? None of us should go. That's what must happen. We should leave well enough alone."

"I didn't get hurt," Tabby said. "But you can't decide for all of us on your own. Quite frankly, I've been dreaming about seeing New York, and seeing it sooner rather than later."

"Perhaps you'll thank me for not bringing you with me to get shot or killed." I was shouting now.

She picked up her tray and stomped off.

Chapter Four

Five minutes later Tabby was back, in a huff.

"If you're going, then I'm coming too. You can't go and see Jules on your own. What would you achieve, other than reading fashion magazines and swooning over stars on Broadway? Well, speaking of that now, it doesn't sound bad at all. To be honest, I'd like to come for that. But you need to think of the treasure as well, Mabel. We're seventeen and we're old enough to decide on things like these. After Jordan, we all know what could happen and if we choose to go anyway you can't stop us." She sat down, knowing in all likelihood that my silence was a sign of encouragement. "We could even sign a statement to the effect that we know the risk but assume responsibility for mishaps or some such thing," she suggested.

"Mishaps? Hugh getting stabbed wasn't a mishap."

"You know what I mean. And I happen to know you love my flair for drama. You think it's funny. That's part of the reason you love me so much," Tabby was enthralled with her own convincing performance.

"I do love you. I just couldn't bear it if anything happened, to you or Barnaby or Hugh. Sometimes it's a heavy weight to bear."

"I know but we can do this. We can be safe. I know we can," she pleaded.

"So, you'd go knowing that Harris might show up and hurt us? That's beyond reckless. How can you even think of it? She's a maniac and he's under her control, or at least I think he is. And we don't even know where he is. That alone is enough to keep us all at home, indefinitely."

"We run that risk every time we cross a street with cars driving down them." Tabby had clearly worked out this argument beforehand. "You need to invite Hugh and Barnaby, clearing it with Jules's family first, and me of course, and we'll all sign something so you can have a free conscience. You can't forbid us to come. You're not the Queen or something like that."

"I knew she'd come into it at some point."

Tabby smiled at me. "So, Madame, will you take us?"

I looked at her. I couldn't not go, but I couldn't take them on another treasure hunt either, not if that might lead us all astray.

"Well?"

"I'm thinking."

"Think faster."

"What's the rush, Tabby? We need to be sure."

"I am sure."

"I know you are, but they're not your birth parents; they're mine."

"And that said," Tabby spread her hands on the table, "we want to come on the treasure hunt. All of us, including Hugh, and if that doesn't say it all, I don't know what will."

I certainly couldn't go without them if they were willing to take the risk.

The Gangster's Fortune

"All right. You win. But everyone needs to sign a paper saying they know the risks. We have to do that, and then I might feel a titch better."

"Of course we will. I knew you'd go for it. So you never told me about the visit. Fill me in on what Grace said."

"The strangest part was that she said she wanted to keep me when I was a baby but they had to hide me from someone and she made it sound like that was the person who took me and put me on the steps of the church. I've been thinking perhaps it was her father and I need to go and find him. Maybe he can explain too, why she turned into a complete nutter."

"The apple might not fall that far from the tree," Tabby said. "Where do you think he might be?"

"I've no idea, but they probably lived in London, somewhere close to the church. I wonder if he's still there."

"He sounds like someone you ought not to be seeing."

"But he's my grandfather, Tabby."

The Gangster's Fortune

"He'd be awful, even worse than she is, if that's how she's turned out. How can you even think of things like this, Mabel?"

"I don't get the feeling she's going to give up either. She's obsessed with me and that makes her very dangerous."

"I understand, really I do. Stealing from us in Scotland, stabbing Hugh in Jordan, making your life a living hell. It's been really hard. But better times are ahead. I can feel it in my bones."

"I don't in mine." I felt glum and confused about Hugh.

"That's because I'm more intuitive than you are."

"You're right on that count. Thanks, Tabby."

"For what?"

"For wanting to do this again. It means more than you know."

And that was because going on an adventure made me feel more like myself than anything else. When we were following clues and getting close to finding something precious I never felt insecure, hopeless, or full of despair. Treasure hunting brought out the best in me. And there was no getting around that.

+++

The four of us sat at Gatwick Airport waiting to board our plane to New York. Once our parents had agreed it was our choice to go, because we were practically adults now, Tabby had us all sign the declaration she'd drafted and everyone felt quite excited about the treasure hunting part of the trip. Hugh and I had spoken briefly a few times on the phone and then we'd met for a soft drink on Lymington High Street.

I walked into the restaurant and saw him already sitting there. Over at the table I felt butterflies rush up inside me.

"Hello," I said, pulling the chair out and sitting down.

"Hello yourself," he said. "How's everything?"

"The tickets are booked. Are you quite sure you want to come, because we have forty-eight hours to change our minds?"

The Gangster's Fortune

"I'm quite sure," he said.

"But how can you be so sure?" I asked. "I know we've talked about it before, but really, you don't have to prove anything to anyone, least of all me."

"I'm not trying to prove anything. I want to come and see if we can find Dutch Schultz's treasure. That's all."

"Right, we don't have much to go on, not like last time, having the map and all."

"But we didn't know the map could help us then. We just thought it might. It was fun though, wasn't it? Traipsing around the desert."

He smiled and then, as if remembering what had happened, he looked sad.

"Yes, it was." I wanted to go back there, I wished we'd never left. I wished things could be the same. That we could be the same.

"Tabby said Barnaby's coming, he seems like a good sort."

"He is. Just like Tabby, only less show-offy. If that's even a word."

The Gangster's Fortune

"I asked the waitress to bring us some Cokes. They should be here soon."

I didn't know what to say. I'd never been speechless with Hugh before. The drinks came and we talked about school and when we got up to leave, he paid the bill, and we walked to the door together and stepped outside.

"This is it then, I suppose," I said. "I hope it's the right thing and you don't hate me afterwards."

"I could never hate you, Mabel. You must know that by now."

"That's nice to hear. I'll see you then."

"See you." He walked away and I'd never felt more alone.

+++

The night before our flight was due to leave, my dad stood quietly at my door. "I'll miss you, Mabel," he said. "Don't give the boys any reason to fight over you."

"Dad, it's not like that."

The Gangster's Fortune

"You forget, Mabel, I used to be one of the boys, with a motorbike and a leather jacket. Why do you think I got into police work? I had an edge once too. Don't you break their hearts and don't let them break yours."

"Thanks for that, Dad." I knew he meant well.

"Dad," I said, as he turned to leave, "there's something I want to ask you to do for me. Could you find Harris before we come back from New York, find him and put him away for a very long time? I can't help thinking that he's already there waiting for us, doing her bidding."

"We don't think Harris is capable of thinking that far ahead. He's demonstrated his loyalty to Grace when she's there to supervise him, but from what we can tell he's not the sharpest tool in the shed. I think without her to tell him what to do, he's not much of a threat on his own. Now if somehow Grace gets out of prison, then we will have a problem."

"I think you're being naïve, Dad. He's a threat too."

"Duly noted, now you try to get some sleep."

The Gangster's Fortune

"One last thing, Dad."

"What is it, Mabel?"

"Do you think you could find out if Grace has a father who's still alive and where he lives? I'd like to know. He's my grandfather and he might be able to answer some questions for me."

"I can try," Dad said, "but this could be very dangerous territory. Stealing a baby takes a special kind of character. You know that, Mabel."

"Yes, but the baby was me. What was he doing, protecting me from her? I really want to find out. Please say you'll help while I'm away so when I come back I can go and find more answers."

"I'll look into it Mabel. Because you've asked. But please just try to enjoy yourself in New York. You're not to worry about anything. Grace is behind bars and her father is probably long dead." He switched off the overhead light from the door.

"When you're in my shoes, Mabel, you can be the judge. Good night, my dear. Now you get some rest."

That was the problem. My police officer father had underestimated Grace and Harris

The Gangster's Fortune

Walker at every turn and because of that she grew stronger and more unpredictable. Despite being in prison, there was no doubt in my mind that she was prepared to do anything to leave my life in tatters. To fell anyone and everyone that mattered to me. It had started with Hugh and in my heart of hearts I knew it wouldn't end there.

When we were at the airport Tabby decided to give us a crash course on the history of New York City and acted out various scenes from the city's history, such as when France donated the Statue of Liberty, playing the Frenchman who famously said of the statue that it "portrays liberty illuminating zee world".

"There was a great blizzard too," Tabby said, "in 1888, that brought nearly two feet of snow and closed the whole city down. The East River was so thick with ice that people could actually walk across it to get to Brooklyn. I wonder how far that is? I expect Jules will show us."

The boys put their headphones on, which I felt like doing too, but that would have been plain rude. So I listened, and when we boarded the plane both boys were more than happy to help lift our cases into the luggage compartments. How we decided who would sit beside whom on the seven-hour journey was another matter.

Tabby had arranged the seating because she'd booked the tickets (with the help of my mum, who through her job had managed free tickets for the boys), and she said the boys should sit together so they could get to know each other. They'd come to my house so they could be introduced to each other and to see if we could all get along all right, and there had been a few outings to go to the films, but they hadn't spent much time alone together and I wondered what they would say to each other, given the chance.

Tabby told how in the 1800s New York had been one big swamp with rocky outcroppings and stagnant ponds, overrun with animals and thousands of wild dogs. Thousands of trees were planted, hills were created, and water brought in to form great lakes. Boulders were moved to form Central Park and the crowning achievement was the Metropolitan Museum of Art.

The Gangster's Fortune

"Now let me tell you about Times Square," Barnaby said, not to be outdone by his sister. "It started with the construction of the *New York Times* newspaper headquarters. Some people called it the Great White Way because of all the bright lights adorning the buildings."

"That's where I want to go," Tabby said.

"The subway opened in 1904 and an accident broke all the windows in Grand Central Station. They built the Chrysler building in 1930." He showed me a page with a photo from his book about the city. "Quite something, isn't she? The design is called Art Deco because of the chrome top and all the gargoyles."

"You do sound like a journalist, or maybe a professor," I said.

"I do?" Barnaby laughed. "I've been wishing you'd say that ever since we met."

"What, when I was fourteen?"

"Maybe not quite that far back. Your hair was different then. You were different then."

I was trying to forget my awkward early teen years too. Would he even have liked me at all if

Hugh hadn't first? I chased those thoughts away and tried to listen.

"Anyway, it was the Dutch who first colonized the area, calling it New Amsterdam. But soon afterwards it became a British colony." He took a map out of his book, unfolded it and showed me Manhattan, which is the island that the city part of New York is on. All the suburbs, like Harlem and the Bronx, are reached by bridges from the main island. As Barnaby pointed this all out I couldn't stop looking at his forearms.

"Then in 1776 they declared their independence and there was a lot of fighting against us, they really didn't like us being there at all. And that's why Canada is still a British colony but America isn't. And now, unfortunately, it's a bit of a cess pool. Lots of crime and drugs. I wonder if your father knows that. But what's interesting is that in the 1950s they tried to run highways right through the middle of the city and knocked down public housing to rebuild the city."

"Did it work?" I asked.

The Gangster's Fortune

"Up to a point. They did demolish this incredible building called Penn Station and that was that. People started protesting and stopped the demolition to keep the villages as they were. There are places called Greenwich Village and the East Village that are like towns within the city and most people who live there don't have a car because there's nowhere to park. And some people live in these great big brick buildings called brownstones in the villages."

"There are doormen at every building. And now there's all this crime. I don't expect we'll be going into the subway anytime soon. It's famous for all the graffiti and looks more like a film set than a place for transporting people."

"I'd like to see it," Hugh said, "and Washington Square Park, it's supposed to be like the Wild West there. Didn't Jules say she was going to take us out of the city to their family's cabin?"

"That's where the treasure is supposed to be hidden, in a place called the Catskills," Tabby said, returning and taking back her seat.

The Gangster's Fortune

When Barnaby had sat back down in his own seat I heard Hugh say quietly, "and may the best man win." I pretended I hadn't heard. What was I thinking, bringing them both?

"You look like you've seen a ghost," Tabby said.

"No, I was just thinking about bringing both the boys," I whispered. "I don't think Hugh's going to throw himself on the sword twice for a girl who's dating someone else."

"I'd be surprised if he didn't," Tabby said. She put on her night mask and drifted off to sleep.

+++

We circled above the city in the early July afternoon sun. With the time difference, we had left London only a few hours after we were due to arrive. After we deboarded the plane, we followed the arrival signs. Barnaby took my hand and Tabby and Hugh walked on ahead. I was pleased Barnaby had come.

The Gangster's Fortune

We reached the arrivals area and saw Jules holding a big sign that read "MABEL HARTLEY YOU'VE ARRIVED." We picked up our bags from the carousel and she hugged and kissed us all, in her high-heeled boots and mini-skirt, with huge white plastic-rimmed glasses and a sheer green top with a black bra underneath.

"Hugh, you're alive!" she said and gave him a big hug.

"Tabby, looking fit as ever," and then she set eyes on me and Barnaby. "Times really have changed, haven't they? Come here or I'll feel so silly holding this big sign for you."

I hugged her fiercely. The last time we'd set eyes on each other, Hugh and I had been carried over the crowd to meet a car that would take us out of Petra in Jordan.

"I'm so glad you see you, really I am." She started crying, but wiping the tears away, she said, "and yet, you still haven't introduced me to your new friend. Barnaby, is it?"

Barnaby smiled at Jules and accepted her hug. Then she whispered to me, "I haven't seen such a fine man in a very long time." I laughed to myself. She hadn't changed a bit.

"Come, come, how many bags do you have? Oh, I forgot, Tabby packs for the moon, doesn't she? Barnaby, when Tabby came to Jordan she packed everything she owned and we didn't get along at all, did we? But then she warmed to me. Most people do. Now the limo is waiting outside and I can't wait to get you all home."

"I think we've got everything," Hugh said. "Lead the way, Jules."

She marched on ahead of us. Her skirt was even shorter from behind and she put a huge felt hat on her head and set a quick pace. I saw Barnaby's eyes travel up the back of her legs.

"She's quite a girl, isn't she?" he said.

I saw Hugh look back at us.

"We're coming, not to worry," I said.

The black limo seemed to have as many doors as windows and a moon roof so we could see the sky as we were driving along. Jules positioned herself between Hugh and Barnaby and introduced us to George, her driver, who looked to

The Gangster's Fortune

be about retirement age. Jules whispered that he was a Latino and raised the glass between him and us, which seemed rather rude to me.

"What have you brought this time, Mabel? A map in your bag, again?"

'No such luck," I said. We rolled down all the windows, and Jules promptly told us to roll them back up again. Didn't we know about the damp? It would ruin her hair in seconds. I wondered what it would do to my hair. I put my cap back on and started looking out of the window, as we merged on to the motorway and then crossed many bridges made of steel with buses, taxis and cars weaving in and out of the lanes.

The sky was overcast and I was glad I had shorts on. We all did, except for Jules, and as we came closer to the city we began to see the soaring skyscrapers, and then we went through a tunnel and seemed to come out in the heart of the asphalt jungle. We waited for a long time in the traffic.

"So, what should I tell you about my city?" Jules asked, opening a sparkling water and offering us each one, which we happily accepted.

The Gangster's Fortune

"As you can see, the safest way to travel is in here with George. You wouldn't believe what they report on the news. There's no real crime where we are, and Chinatown's pretty good too. And Ronald Reagan is our President and the mayor is trying to clean up the city with a zero tolerance on crime. We'll stay away from Washington Square Park, while you're here, that really is the one of the worst places for drugs. People have crack pipes in wads of tissue paper and bang their heads on the sidewalk. It's pretty disturbing. It could be quite nice if it wasn't for that. There's an Arc de Triumph like the one in Paris there and the city has so many secret places to explore. I suppose they're not secret to those of us who live here, but to visitors they are. Tomorrow, we'll go to the Metropolitan Museum, that in itself is worth a visit to New York City."

"Now, tell me, what's been going on? Your letters take far too long to get here but I am thrilled you've arrived. I've been looking forward to it for months. And I mean months."

The Gangster's Fortune

"How are things at home for you?" I asked. "Are your parents really all right with us coming, after what happened in Petra?"

"About that," Tabby said. "I've drafted a letter that we've all signed, saying we know the risks involved in coming and you just have to sign yours, Jules. I have the paper in my bag. You should sign now to get it over with, then Mabel will have a clear conscience."

"Is that really necessary?" Jules sounded irritated.

"Mabel wanted it because she says Harris is still on the loose and could be a threat to all our safety," Tabby said.

"Do you really feel that way?" Jules said.

"You know I do, I wrote to you about it in one of my letters."

"Oh, right. Now I remember. But your mother's in jail and he's not much of a threat on his own, is he?"

"Nobody thinks so but me," I said. "And I gather your parents are of the same mind?"

The Gangster's Fortune

"Thanks to you, Mabel, my parents actually seem to like having me around."

Tabby produced the paper and Jules signed.

"Mom especially loves telling her friends that I was part of finding the treasure in Petra. It's all changed and I couldn't be happier. The boys have gone to the Hamptons for the summer on condition that I got to take you to the house in the Catskills. It's actually more of a cottage, but we'll have a car to use and George will stay here with mother. It's all been settled. Not long now," she said.

We looked out again, and saw the city went on forever, block after block of towers. You could see why people came here. There was so much to see and I liked that parts of it were older and had history like England.

The Gangster's Fortune

Chapter Five

George pulled to a stop in front of a building that looked like a hotel. "Now that," Jules said, as we were getting out with our bags, "is Central Park. We can picnic there, and go for walks and ride bikes and it's just the most wonderful place on earth and when you're in it you don't feel like you're in the middle of New York City at all, you just feel like you're in nature and it goes on forever. We can see a view of it from the apartment. Now we'll have to see about sleeping, where everyone's going to go, but with my brothers gone, there's more room, and my step-father's away on business and Mom's forever at board meetings and lunches so we'll be left quite to ourselves for the time you're here."

"Thank you, George," I said, introducing myself. George could have been a bodyguard, judging from his size, and I wondered if that was part of his job description.

"This is Tabitha Mason, her brother Barnaby and Hugh McGinley. Thank you for driving us."

The Gangster's Fortune

"I've never met anyone from England before," he said, his voice was deep and very gentle. He wore a chauffeur's black cap and a black suit with a tie.

"Have you always lived in New York?" I asked.

"Born and raised, and with Jules and her family for many years now. Please call on me for anything you need. I have a phone in the car. I'm at your service."

We went in past a doorman in uniform with a burgundy blazer with gold cords on the shoulders, a hat that matched, grey trousers and black shoes. We made our way to the front desk.

"Jules," a security guard said.

"This is Hugh, Tabby, Mabel and Barnaby. They're from England and they're going to be staying with me. Please don't give them a hard time about coming and going. They're my friends and I know you'll make them all feel welcome."

"Welcome," said the security guard with the name tag Fred. He asked Jules to sign a paper attached to a clip board and she had to write all our

The Gangster's Fortune

names down with the number of their flat. He took each of us, and pointed out the cameras in the corners of the ceilings. I wondered how many of Jules' other friends had brought trouble into the building.

We rode up in a very posh lift: it looked as if the panel and all the buttons were made of gold. We stopped on the 68th floor, the penthouse, and got out. The door opened right into the living area. We all looked at each other, feeling a little stunned. How had she managed to spend months in the dirt and caves we'd lived in in Jordan? It was no wonder she'd wanted to go home as soon as she'd come.

"Now let me show you where you'll be. Mabel and Tabby, you're in the room next to mine, we'll be sharing a bathroom, and the boys will share down the hall there.'

"Valentia! We're home," Jules shouted, and a tiny woman, who looked to be in her fifties, appeared in a maid's uniform with a white hat and apron and a grey dress underneath. "Valentia, these are my friends." She introduced us all again.

The Gangster's Fortune

We went to find our rooms, changed and then gathered back by the lift.

"We're going to see Times Square first, tonight, I mean because it's absolutely fabulous and Tabby you will love it, because all the plays on Broadway happen right there and we'll just go and have a walk around then come home."

Times Square really was beyond belief. The fluorescent advertising five or six stories high went up all the buildings. It was like being at a carnival, and I loved it. There were people dressed up like the Statue of Liberty to have photos taken with. There were strongmen only in swimming trunks, with the American flag on them, and a cowboy hat and boots, also willing to pose with tourists for a price.

Tabby had to get her picture with him and said she'd never have believed it if she hadn't seen it for herself. Times Square itself was full of trinket shops and people trying to sell theatre tickets and George came with us because he said he'd been directed to keep an eye on us all. I didn't envy him his job.

The Gangster's Fortune

Tabby and I walked together and Jules linked arms with the boys and told them which Broadway shows she'd been to and it sounded like she'd seen all of them twice. The Broadway District was down another street, away from Times Square, and we walked into a shop and got some New York cheesecake at a small take-away. Going back to Times Square, I decided how very much I liked New York. She had such a pulse and I couldn't believe we were lucky enough to have made it here. It felt electric in the city that never sleeps and I couldn't get over how many people there were doing odd jobs, I supposed, just trying to make a living.

"We'll come back again, but the first sighting really is the best." Jules followed George back to the car.

When we got back to her flat we all said goodnight and I wondered how the boys would fare in their room but I was too tired even to say goodnight to Tabby. We flopped into bed and hours later I was wide-awake. I wondered if it was the jet-lag that was keeping me up. I wandered out to the kitchen to get some hot milk and saw someone asleep on the sofa in the living room.

"Mabel," I heard and looked over. It was Hugh, sitting up. My heart thundered in my chest.

"You startled me, what are you doing out here?"

"Couldn't sleep. Barnaby was snoring."

"Sorry," I said. "Would you like some milk?"

"Yes, please."

When I'd heated up two cups, I brought them over and we sat on the couch in the dark sipping our drinks.

"How are you, Hugh?" I asked. His shirt was off and he had blankets gathered around his middle and covering his legs. I tried not to look at him but it was hard not to.

The moon was bright in the sky, and shone through the huge windows. It wasn't hard to see him at all and I wished there was more cover of night to hide his body. I couldn't be sure how I looked either.

"Can't believe we're here. Ever seen so many lights as at Times Square? It was kind of charming, in a very American way. I'm not sure if charming is the right word but I liked it." I was blabbering, not knowing what to say but well aware we were alone.

"It's all right. You don't have to stay out here with me, you know."

But I can't tear myself away, that's what I wanted to say but I couldn't.

"Do you think we'll ever be the way we used to be again? I feel like everything's changed for us."

"It has, Mabel," he sipped his milk.

I felt my eyes start to tear up.

"Don't cry," he said putting his hand on my face.

"I'm not crying. I'm just tired," I lied, inching away from him.

Then I felt consumed by anger and I wanted to lash out at him.

"You did this. You made us like this."

"I did this?" He looked at me in amazement.

"By not talking to me all year. By leaving me."

"What on earth are you talking about?" He looked mystified. "I stayed at Hollingsworth so I could be with you. I could have left but I wanted to be able to see you, at the very least."

"I don't want to fight."

"You could've fooled me."

"I've been so lonely."

"So have I, Mabel."

"Why did you do it, Hugh? No one asked you to risk your life by getting into the helicopter in Jordan."

"She would have taken you away and I'd never have seen you again. I needed to protect you. I would have done anything for you."

"And now? You'll come to New York and pretend you haven't any feelings for me?" My voice was shaking.

"She's in prison. She can't get to you and we're here as friends, Mabel. Nothing more. You've seen to that by bringing Barnaby." His voice was rising in anger too.

"You're angry because I've moved on?"

"Moved on? You've done far more than that, you've brought him to New York to share a room with me."

The Gangster's Fortune

I agreed, it didn't sound the best. "Now you've got a clean line of sight to Jules." I hated myself for saying it but what did I want?

"If you really believe that, Mabel, you have no idea. You think everything could go back to normal after that stabbing?"

I looked at his chest and the scar I'd never seen before, which ran in a line from his collarbone to his armpit.

'I never believed what she might be capable of. Or how much it would cost me."

He reached out and took my hand. We both sat back as he put my hand on the scar that would never go away and would always come between us now.

"What happened to us?" I said.

"You stopped believing in me."

"You stopped giving me a reason to believe."

"You could have waited."

"For what?"

"For this." He leaned in to kiss me and put his hand up on my cheek and I felt his lips on mine and I felt his breath and his skin and the blonde whiskers on his face that I'd longed to touch and as he pulled me close, all the love came rushing back, all the love I'd felt for him.

"We can't do this," I said pulling away. "I can't do this. Goodnight, Hugh." I walked to bed feeling dazed and giddy and confused and thought about Barnaby and a fresh start and told myself that being close with Hugh could never, ever happen again.

+++

In the morning, Jules and Tabby were at the end of my bed. It had satin sheets and everything in the room was one or another tone of grey. Tabby had drawn the floor-to-ceiling silk curtains and the sun was streaming through the window.

"I'm scared to touch anything, Jules," Tabby said.

"I know, I was too when we moved here, but you'll get used to it."

Beside the windows in our room was a dresser with a large mirror, and a chair in front of it

The Gangster's Fortune

that you could sit on when you brushed your hair and put on your make-up.

Tabby pounced on it. "I feel famous already," she giggled.

'The boys have gone to get bagels, with George," Jules said. "And Mom's up. She was in bed when we got home last night, and wants you to come now. We shouldn't keep her waiting."

I wasn't sure about being summoned to the kitchen, but we were guests so I thought we'd best do whatever we could to ensure a pleasant stay. Jules handed me a grey silk robe that went down to my ankles and gave one to Tabby too. Jules was wearing fuchsia silk men's pyjamas and looked like she'd just come back from an hour at the beauty salon.

She was so beautiful, with long legs, long blonde hair, a perfect face, and mouth with lovely big lips. She looked like she'd already spent hours on the chair in front of the mirror. I longed to look like her. But I didn't really like mirrors, except when I was getting my hair done, and then I suppose I looked all right.

The Gangster's Fortune

"Let's go, it's late and Mom's got a luncheon she needs to get to in half an hour."

We left our room and went into the living area. The outside walls were all glass and we could see down to Central Park.

"I'm Vivian," Jules' mum said, reaching out her very long, manicured hand with its long, red painted nails. She was as tall as Jules, with blonde hair that was parted in the middle and fell in feathered locks to her shoulder blades in a blunt cut. She wore what looked like a black and white Chanel suit, with lots of bangles on her arms and rings on her fingers.

"Mabel Hartley and Tabitha Mason," she said, "You have no idea how long I've been waiting to meet you. Jules came home from the archaeological dig in Jordan a whole different girl. Jules has become, much to our astonishment, a straight A student and is going to NYU to study archaeology next fall. We're all quite astounded and we have you both to thank."

"NYU?" I asked.

The Gangster's Fortune

"New York University," Jules whispered. She seemed a bit scared to speak out of turn around her mum, which I thought was very curious, seeing that Jules was notorious (at least amongst us) for her brash nature.

'And, I must say, it is a bit of a relief that the person who hurt Hugh in Jordan is behind bars. We are all quite relieved to say the least. So what do you think you might want to do while you're here?" Vivian asked, taking a make-up compact out of her black snakeskin handbag. She powdered her nose and then applied a layer of red lipstick to her lip. "I imagine you're quite tired from the flight, but you don't have to really do very much at all. Something Julia used to be quite good at. A little too good at, but she's reformed her ways. Let Julia be your hostess and of course the house in the Catskills is yours to visit when you get tired of the city. Please help yourself to anything in the fridge and enjoy. It's wonderful that Julia has proper friends to come and see her!"

The Gangster's Fortune

Then she air-kissed both sides of Jules face and said she would have George most of the afternoon but she would be home for dinner.

+++

After putting in a few solid hours at the Metropolitan Museum of Art the next morning, we found a food trolley in Central Park and we all lay about in the grass. It was a beautiful day. I was thinking about how quickly we could get out of the city and make our way to finding the treasure when Hugh said, "Does anyone know anything about Dutch Schultz anyway?"

"No need to ask, it's all up here," Tabby said, tapping the side of her forehead. Hugh rolled his eyes as he always did when Tabby was preparing one of her lectures, and I had to smile.

"He was born here in New York City in 1902 and his original name was Arthur Flegenheimer but he was given the name Dutch Schultz after he committed his first crime, when he was just seventeen. He didn't have a long life ahead of him.

The Gangster's Fortune

In 1935, when he was thirty-three, he was shot and killed in a restaurant in Newark, which is just over the river from New York. By that time he had been involved in numerous gangland wars, had fought the US government on tax evasion issues, and had amassed a fortune through various criminal operations. When his second tax evasion trial opened, it looked as if he would be serving time, so he took seven million dollars, put it in a safe, drove to upstate New York, and buried it somewhere secret so he'd have a nest egg when he got out."

"And that's what we're doing here, well, not in Central Park but in New York, looking for the treasure," I said, feeling good that we were finally coming to the real reason we'd come on the trip to New York. It seemed awfully long in coming this time. I hoped things would feel less complicated once we left the city and could pursue treasure hunting in earnest.

"And the only people who knew where the safe was buried were his bodyguards, who helped him dig the hole," Barnaby said. "I was reading

Tabby's notes while she practised that performance."

"Barnaby, would you stop?" Tabby turned bright red and put her sunglasses on.

Ignoring his sister, Barnaby continued. "But they were all gunned down inside The Palace Chop House. On his death bed, Schultz began hallucinating and rambling. Some people believed that his incoherent references were about something hidden in the woods in Phoenicia, which is where Jules' family has their house, so it couldn't be better."

"And where's Phoenicia, Jules?" Hugh asked. She came over and knelt beside him. She was wearing a flowery print sheath dress, cowboy boots and a floppy straw hat, and sunglasses on the bridge of her nose.

"Not far. My dad has another car we can use and seeing as *you know who* just got her license, I'll be driving," Jules put her head on Hugh's shoulder. "But only if you all promise to let me have the radio up as loud as I want, and you all have to sing with me or I can't possibly drive without getting in an accident. Those are my terms. So we'll drive for about two and a half hours north to the Catskill Mountains. You'll love it. We'll get out of here. But not quite yet."

Here wasn't so bad at all. I loved Central Park. We'd walked so far into it that it was hard to believe you were right in the middle of a city, unless you looked up to the outer edges of the park and then you could see the buildings.

"By some accounts Schultz's nest egg was all in money and bonds, while other accounts have it as double-eagle gold pieces, and others say it's a combination of cash and jewels that were stuffed into tobacco sacks," Tabby said.

"You really are thorough, aren't you? Boringly so."

Tabby glared at Jules as she stretched out her long legs and crossed them in front of her. "I like to read, and Schultz is all over the encyclopaedias," she said. "My parents have every collection known to man. At one point on his death bed, Schultz asked Lulu - that was his bodyguard's name - to drive him back to Phoenicia. He also said, "We'd better get those liberty bonds out of the box and cash 'em."

Tabby did her best gangster voice, made her fingers into a pistol and blew on the tip of it. "And he said something about the Devil Girl. That was pretty odd."

"What about the Devil Girl?" Hugh perked up.

"That's all I know," Tabby said.

Hugh started clapping. I shot him a look. "Now we all know you're the smartest Tabby, as usual."

"Hugh," I started to say but it wasn't my place any more, was it?

"No, you're right, I'm just giving Tabby a hard time, aren't I? Some things do stay the same."

The Gangster's Fortune

Chapter Six

A few days later, after playing tourists for much longer than I'd have liked, we packed all our things into her dad's Jaguar and set off for the Catskill Mountains. Jules was driving and Tabby was in the front seat beside her, with a map she had drawn our route on.

We weren't far out of New York before Jules asked the dreaded question. I was sitting between the boys in the back seat. We were packed in like sardines, the radio was blaring, and Jules was singing her heart away. Then she stopped and turned the radio off.

"So, just to be clear," she said, as we drove out of the city. She rolled down her window and let her hair dangle out of it. "You haven't had any messages from your birth mother in prison have you, Mabel? Or anyone else that's been in contact with her?"

I almost coughed up the fizzy drink I'd been sucking on. "No, why do you ask?"

"Because last time you got that note from her, and we decided to stay. Remember when we were swimming in that salty lake in Israel?"

"It was called the Dead Sea," Tabby said.

Jules ignored Tabby. "And we got that weird note from her, like she was spying on us, and we stayed and didn't tell anyone. I just want to make sure we're not repeating that. I don't want Hugh to get hurt again, just saying. Or Barnaby, for that matter," she glanced back at him in her mirror.

"I didn't know about the Dead Sea note," Barnaby said.

"You can't know everything," Hugh said.

"So, anything, Mabel?" Jules insisted.

"No, honestly I can say nothing. Not a word since we saw her in England."

"Well, that's a relief. I felt sure you were going to pull something out of your pocket," Jules said. "Now we can relax."

Barnaby put his hand on my shoulder. "We're quite safe," he said. "And nothing even remotely scary happened in New York, really, we seem to be on a roll."

The Gangster's Fortune

Hugh wasn't looking at me. He was scanning his sketchbook. The night before he'd shown us some sketches of Jules at the Empire State Building looking through one of the telescopes out over the city.

There were others in his sketchbook of the Chrysler Building and the day we'd gone back to the Metropolitan Museum and had been to the sculpture gallery to see the Rodin sculptures. We'd spent at least an hour there, with Hugh sketching the famous sculpture called *The Kiss* where a woman sitting beside a man has her arm up around his neck. His arm is on her hip and they are locked in a kiss.

"It's my favourite," Hugh had said to me. "They just look so devoted to each other. Like they'll always be like that."

Barnaby had been off looking at the sculpture of the naked nymph playing the gold harp with Jules and Tabby.

"Do you think we'll ever be like that again?" Hugh asked.

"We were never like *that*," I said, smiling.

"But I always thought we would be, one day," Hugh said.

In the car, Hugh shut his notebook abruptly and rolled down his window. We drove on, escaping the city, and driving into the hills.

"Should we think about Dutch Schultz? What are we going to do first?" I asked.

"We should probably settle in. What's your house like?" Tabby asked Jules.

"It's the house my mom grew up in. It's on a quiet little stream in a big field and there always seem to be lots of geese on the lawn near the pond. We have a couple of bedrooms and it's a lot simpler than where we live in the city. But Mom can't give it up. She says there are too many memories there. She grew up in Phoenicia. She's tried to find the Dutch Schultz treasure herself."

"And?" Tabby said.

"No luck. Everybody's tried to find it there. I don't think there's many places to look that haven't been gone over by everyone," Jules said.

The Gangster's Fortune

"I think I'll be ready for a walk when we get there," I said, feeling cramped and stuffy in the car. "Are there woods around the cabin?"

"More than you could imagine," Jules said. "We used to have parties in the bushes. I just never really made it out of them. You know how I was."

I remembered a girl who had prescription medicine in her bag that she'd taken from her mother and brought to Jordan to help her 'get through'. I'd made her drop it down the toilet and that was when we became friends, because she thought she needed the drugs but she didn't.

She looked at me in the mirror and smiled. I remembered what a soft heart she had and how she wanted everyone to think she was so experienced but really, she just wanted people to like her.

"There's lots of streams, and green. You are going to love it. Not long now, a few more winding roads and we'll have everything we need. I hope you won't get bored."

"Bored, with you Jules?" Hugh said, "never."

The Gangster's Fortune

There was mist on the pond behind the house and driving in along a dirt road, we passed an alley of trees with long grass.

When we made it to the cottage, I could see Jules was right, it was just a cabin in the woods, nothing fancy, just the kind of place you'd want to go and unwind with your *two* boyfriends and two best friends who didn't get along with each other.

"You know this is the tubing capital of the world," she said, popping the boot when we got to the house so we could get our bags out. Jules took the key out from under the mat.

"Tubing?" Tabby asked.

"You know, when you float down the river on a rubber tube, like a tire," Jules said. "But with more rapids, people get bruises if they're not careful."

"Can we do that?" Barnaby said. "I'd love to try it."

"Course we can, if we can get the treasure hunters to take a day off. There's a first time for everything in Phoenicia," Jules said.

The cottage was on the outskirts of the town and Jules said we'd go in later to pick up food supplies when we ran out of what we'd brought from the apartment. It was a house with white boards on the outside and black trim.

"The creek beside the house is called Little Wappinger's Creek," Jules said. She had her country fashion on, with boots, jeans, and a t-shirt tied up in a knot above her waist showing off a very tanned, flat tummy. She had a cap on that was crocheted and I thought she might be wearing fake eyelashes now as her eyes looked very startling with smoky makeup. What was she doing with us English fuddy-duddies I thought?

There was a large stone chimney at the front of the house and a set of double doors on the right, beside the chimney. Once inside, we saw two windows at ground level that looked out from a cozy living area, with a wooden coffee table in the middle. There was a large kitchen with wooden cupboards. I wondered which one of us would be doing the cooking. There were bedrooms with no curtains beside the windows.

"There's a keystone bridge out on the property, too," Jules said as we brought our bags in. "Tabby and Mabel, you're in here, and boys, you're in the next room."

"Where are you sleeping, Jules?" Tabby asked.

"I've got a spot in the attic," she winked at Hugh when she said it and I went to lie down.

"Are you all right?" Barnaby poked his head in the door. "You wanted to go for a walk, didn't you?"

"I think I need a cup of tea first," I said. "You know it just feels a little bit funny being in the middle of nowhere. I want to be looking for something."

"You mean you want a distraction." He came over and brushed the hair back from my eyes. "I think all this treasure hunting takes the place of you living an ordinary life."

"You're probably right. We're probably not going to find anything this time and I was feeling bad about that, but right now, it feels as if it might be all right just to have a holiday."

"Mind if I lie down beside you? No funny business, I promise."

The Gangster's Fortune

"Get the blanket that's at the bottom of the bed," I said, and he pulled it up and lay down on the bed beside me. Then he put his arm around my shoulders and we cuddled underneath it.

"I did bring you something," Barnaby said, slipping his hand in his back pocket. "I picked it up when we were getting petrol." He handed me a brochure. On the front it said *Heron's Drift*.

"We might find something there," Barnaby said, "it's on Main Street, in the centre of Phoenicia. Look, we can visit a creepy doll exhibit or marvel at Petey the Petrified Piranha."

'Sounds like we're on the trail of something big," I said snuggling up against him. He took the brochure from me. "There's a 1950s children's drawing of the many moods of Goofy, you know, from Mickey Mouse? I think we could have a lot of fun there, don't you?"

I had a headache that made the left side of my head ache. It felt as if there was a tiny little man standing on the inside of my eyeball with a little hammer, hitting my eye with it. "I think I have a migraine," I said.

"What's wrong with Mabel?" Tabby said, coming in.

"She's got a migraine."

"I'll leave you," she said. "Feel better soon. Anything I can get you?"

"Nothing," I said.

"We're going to go for a walk, want to come?" she asked.

I shook my head.

"Barnaby?"

"No, I'll stay with Mabel."

We heard them leave the house about ten minutes later with a slamming of the back door.

"All alone at last," Barnaby said. "You know we haven't been alone since we left England? You really do everything as a group, don't you?"

I nodded. "Is that such a bad thing?"

"No, just not what I expected."

He came back and lay down under the blanket, putting his arm under my head and kissing my temple. He turned to face me and ran his finger down my cheek. Then he pulled me close to him until we were lying so close he could have kissed me, but instead he just lay beside me, smoothing my hair and tracing my face with his fingers.

"I love you, Mabel," he said. "You don't have to say it back to me, I know it's a hard thing to say and you've probably never said it before, but I just wanted you to know. Because I haven't felt this way before, really never, and well that's it."

I opened my eyes and looked at Barnaby.

"What?" he said. "Have I screwed everything up? Oh, I have, haven't I?"

"No, it's sweet. It's wonderful. Thank you. I just can't say it back."

The little hammer started going in my eye again.

"Why not?"

I couldn't believe he was asking. "Barnaby," I said, "it's just too soon for me. I don't know what to say." I shut my eyes and felt tears sting the corners.

"I didn't say it to make you cry," he said. "I thought it might make you happy. I just want you to be happy. And I'll do anything."

"Just hold me close to you," I said. "I'm sorry." I started to sob. Then the tears really started to flow and I kept crying.

"Shh, shh, shh," Barnaby said. "It's all right. The tears aren't about what I just said, are they?"

"No, not at all. I'm just crying because I felt I needed to, because I can't be what you want me to be."

"You are, Mabel, don't you see? You are perfect in every way. So full of courage and so much the sort of person I want to be with. You're still so young and maybe I shouldn't have come, maybe you can't feel this way about me."

"I can, I do, I just feel torn apart inside."

"Because of Hugh?"

"Because of me, because I only seem to be able to hurt people and I don't want anyone else to be in that position so I can't love again."

"You loved before. You mean Hugh?"

I nodded. "But I'm not sure I do any more. I really don't know."

Barnaby signed and rubbed his forehead. "I had no idea. I just thought. I feel such a fool."

The Gangster's Fortune

"Don't," I said. "It's me. But I love it that you're here and I love being with you. And who knows what could happen given a little more time. If you could just be a little patient with me. And once we get home we can be together, alone, I mean. I was such a fool to think we could all do this."

"So, you're saying there's a strong possibility you could feel something for me?" He brushed my cheek with his hand and I kissed him and pulled myself on top of him until we were lying together kissing. I laughed.

"But you were just crying," he said, kissing me once more. "I'll always want you. It's just that I can't work out why."

I felt better the next morning. We all had breakfast, and settled in. Hugh stayed in his room for most of the morning and Tabby had to go and get him to see if he wanted to come into town with us. They spent quite a while talking until I started to get impatient and yelled, "We're going now," down the hall.

Tabby poked her head out of the door and beckoned for me to come. I walked down, not sure what to expect. Things had been so good with Barnaby, I didn't want to get drawn back into my confused feelings.

"He wants to talk to you," she said whispering. "I tried to get him to come but he won't budge. I think he wants to go home."

"Home? But he can't go home. We only just got here."

Tabby shrugged her shoulders.

"I'll talk to him," I stepped through the doorway and Tabby closed the door behind me.

"Anything I can do?" I sat on the end of his bed.

"I just can't stand it anymore. I thought I could but I can't."

"Maybe you just need a break from the group."

"No, I need a break from you, Mabel. This was the worst idea in the world. I can't stop thinking about you and Barnaby and what you're doing together and how you can be so casual about everything."

The Gangster's Fortune

"Just a moment. I don't want you to go home, Hugh, but I've started something here with Barnaby because you weren't around. And you think it's easy for me to just break it off and hurt him because you might have changed your mind? It's not easy, not by a long shot."

"I know it's not easy." He took my hand in his. "I want you to know that I'm having a tough time."

"Why don't we see how things go in the next forty-eight hours and if you still want to go, we'll change your ticket. I can't bring myself to break Barnaby's heart until we get home. He's never even been out of England before. I can't just send him home like that; it wouldn't be fair."

"I know he's a good person, isn't he? Or you wouldn't like him the way you do."

"I like you both."

"Just like?"

"I like you both," I repeated hoping that saying the words would make it true.

"I never stopped loving you, Mabel. You must know that, and when you are Barnaby are alone, well, it's killing me. Have you?"

"Have we what?"

"You know."

"No, we haven't. We're taking things slowly, just like we did."

"Oh," he said brightening up.

"So that's what this is all about?"

"It's killing me only to watch you and Barnaby fall deeper in love."

"I'm not in love with him," I said. "At least not yet. But he has strong feelings."

"I can see that."

"Promise you'll stay just a day or two more and help us until we find out if there's any way for us to find the gangster's treasure. Truce?" I said, holding out my hand. "And then we'll see what happens when we get home."

He put his hand in mine and pulled me over close to him. "You know, Mabel Hartley, I feel a bit cheered up. I'll stay a few more days."

We joined the others and we all got in the car and headed out to Phoenicia. Jules was a good tour guide. She told us about the places where people had looked for Dutch Schultz's treasure.

The Gangster's Fortune

"There's the Hudler Cemetery, and a lot of people go there, and then there's the Devil Tombstone, which is a large boulder and campground, and it looks like there's a devil in the rock face. The campground opened in the 1920s, so there's a chance it may be there. And Schultz, according to my mom, used to go to the Phoenicia Hotel. It's in the centre of town. And lots of people have gone looking along Route 28, which is what we're heading in on now, along Esopus Creek. Now we're coming into Phoenicia, there's the *Heron's Drift*, that's where you wanted to go, isn't it Mabel?"

The Gangster's Fortune

Chapter Seven

The Main Street in Phoenicia looked like nothing I'd ever seen before. Small villages in England are steeped in history, with old buildings and cobbled streets that you can imagine Roman soldiers marching down over a thousand years ago. The history at home was something I'd often taken for granted and I'd never set foot in a small American town before. At least not one that was full of summer holiday homes for New Yorkers.

It was a sleepy little town, with multi-coloured houses and American flags lining the streets. To call it unremarkable would be true, yet it felt wrong saying so, because there was a certain charm there, something I couldn't quite put my finger on. It actually made me miss my parents.

We hadn't been away for very long, and yet it seemed strange to be on holiday, looking at the hills that rose up behind the town, while at the same time thinking of my father sitting behind his desk, and my mother somewhere in the skies. I felt so far away from them and realized that this was also a taste of things to come, when I would no longer be at Hollingsworth but a student at some university, and I wouldn't come home every weekend but perhaps only see my parents at Christmas and Easter. I was starting to have a sense of what it was like to be a grown-up, or at least someone old enough to look after herself, and it brought a sense of loss, of missing home.

It cost a fortune to make phone calls home and our letters would probably arrive after we did, so I decided to send picture postcards to my mum and dad. I made a mental note to find one of Main Street and send it off without delay. I wanted them to know what it was like and to be able to picture where I was, because I supposed the people here lived quiet lives, nestled in the mountains, knowing their neighbours, as we did at home, so some things were the same.

As we drove through the town, we noticed a huge sculpture of an Indian chief on the lawn, with a Davy Crockett hat on his head, and a gun on his shoulder.

The Gangster's Fortune

"That's it," Tabby pointed from the front seat, "beside the big Indian fellow, see the sign that says *Heron's Drift*. I think that's what we're looking for. Pull over, Jules, would you?"

Jules was an unexpectedly good driver and took pride in parallel parking and making sure the car was looked after. We walked up the front steps, past the large Indian fellow, and past the sign that said we'd find antiques, records, vintage clothing and oddities.

The front porch was full of clothes on hangers on a rolling rack, and inside, stepping through the front door, we saw a room full of records, stacks of them in rows up against the wall, and then on shelves going up another wall.

In the other room on the other side of the house were racks and racks of clothes, lots of dresses that looked like they might have been worn by hippies. There were dresses with bright colours, short hems and costumes for every kind of event and celebration.

I walked down a hall between the two rooms towards a room in the back. On one side was the most extensive collection of porcelain dolls I'd ever seen, with dresses, some stained, with frayed hair and eyes that closed when you laid the doll down. I'd never seen such a collection of oddities before. Above them was the picture of a girl, a framed portrait, but someone had drawn devil's ears on her face. She had creamy brown skin, black plaited hair, and a mischievous smile. I lifted the picture off the wall, and on the back found this inscription: "Meet Desdemona, the devil girl of Phoenicia" and beside that "Not for sale."

We'd all fanned out when we came in and now Hugh joined me in the room with the dolls. There were shelves of books under the dolls and other shelves with a variety of old cameras and film containers on them. I knelt down to look through the books and as I did so I knocked an old set of scales off the bookshelf.

"Hugh, help me, would you? This set of scales is heavier than it looks."

He came right over to help me, as he always did. We both bent down and behind the bookshelf I could see there was a space where it didn't meet the wall, and there on the floor, covered in dust, lay what looked like a notebook. I reached out for it and picked it up out of the dust. It was a child's notebook with a cover made of thick pink cardboard and lots of drawings inside. There was no name on the cover.

"What is it, Mabel?" Hugh asked, putting the scale back on the shelf and peering over my shoulder at the book.

"I don't know. But it's got me wondering."

Flipping through the pages I found a big drawing of a heart with a Cupid's arrow inside it, and as I skimmed further I discovered that it was the diary of a girl called Desdemona. I also found a receipt in it from the Phoenicia Hotel, dated 1933, with devils' ears and a tail drawn on it. I nodded at Hugh to make him look at the photo of the child on the wall, who had the same ears, and the same tail coming out from behind her dress. Hugh said her name under his breath.

"I wonder if it's for sale?" I said. "If they let us take the diary then we might find some clues in it, which means you can't go home yet."

The Gangster's Fortune

"Right, shall we go then? Maybe get a doll too so we can have something else to put on the counter." He looked at the selection of dolls. There was one with black skin, blue eyes and frizzy hair. She wore a faded white dress, and when I turned her over, I saw that a red devil's tail had been sewn into her dress.

"Now that's just too much!" I said.

"I'll get the others," Hugh said, "and you go and pay."

I had some American money. The price of the doll was $15. I put the items on the counter and smiled at the young woman at the cash register who was dressed in a heavy metal t-shirt and ripped jeans, and had tattoos down her arms.

"Oh, I see you found Desdemona's notebook and a doll that looks quite like her. What do you think of the store?"

"It's something so special," I said, taking my money out.

"You've an accent," the woman smiled back at me, taking my money.

The Gangster's Fortune

"Yes, we're from England, visiting our friend from New York. Is there anywhere you'd suggest we could go for lunch?"

She put the doll and the book in a bag and told me to go down the street a few blocks to try the pizzeria. "You'll love it. We all do," and passed me the bag. "It's called Brios."

"I was wondering if you have a moment about this Desdemona. How did her diary come to be here?"

"I've been told that a call was made, this was before my time, of course, to go clean out the house for anything we might want. The collection was hers. Something happened to her mamma and they were never seen again. Tragic. I think she was murdered."

She was whispering now. Her lipstick had worn off and there was a dark red stain from it on her lips and heavy black eyeliner around her eyes. "Not much happens around these parts, so when you hear a story like that, you remember it."

"Who was murdered? Desdemona or her mother?"

The Gangster's Fortune

"The mother," the girl said, with an American drawl. "I think she was a jazz singer in the city. A real character, if you know what I mean. Anyway, enjoy your time here. Neat to meet some English people!"

I thanked her and soon afterwards we left the store.

"Mabel's got something," Hugh told the others as we walked down the street toward the pizza place.

"I know, we saw the doll," Tabby said. "A bit odd if you ask me. What could you possibly want with that, Mabel?"

'I'm not sure. Let's sit down inside, and then we can take a look at it." We walked up the steps to the pizza place and when we were sitting down at the table I opened the book. Instantly I had that familiar rush of reading about past lives that held mystery.

"Let's look through this. Here, there's some writing here. It says, 1930."

The Gangster's Fortune

The nice man came again to see Momma. He comes at night and they talk for hours after I'm supposed to be in bed. But I listen at the door with the dolly he gave me, he calls me his little devil. And I thought that was bad, because the devil is supposed to be bad, but he says no, because I'm his little devil it makes me good.

He says he loves to visit and comes here when he can get away from his business in New York. I asked him how he met my Momma and he says he was the luckiest man in all New York to see her singing in a jazz club. When I asked what a jazz club was he said it was a place for music.

I told him I wanted to come, but he said it was no place for little devils like me. Then he tickled me until I couldn't stop laughing. Momma sent me to bed, but before I went, I sat on his knee and asked him why they call him Dutch and he said because he liked it and it sounded better than his real name Arthur.

"Let's read some more," Tabby said.

The Gangster's Fortune

1931

Dutch comes every Saturday now, and has even bought Momma a new house but we're not on a road with other children, it's just us and miles of woods and a stream and I like it here. Really, I do. I especially like when Dutch comes with porcelain dolls. We never seen anything like these dolls before Dutch came.

I asked Momma if he's my daddy, and she just smiled at me because you see Dutch is white and Momma is black and I'm somewhere in between. Dutch says I'm the most beautiful girl he's ever seen but I must call him Dutch and not Daddy.

Even though he's been coming here ever since I can remember. And now with this new house, he arranged for Momma to have a piano and she's always looking for new things to cook that he might like. Once he came with a friend he called Lulu and they sat with us and both looked very tired. Lulu said I was a very pretty girl with lots of curls and we were very lucky to have such a nice home. I miss Dutch when he doesn't come but he says he's very busy in New York City and tries to come as much as he can.

I flipped a few pages on. "How old do you think she is?" I asked.

"She sounds about ten. She certainly reads and writes well. But why would they be stuck in a big farmhouse out here in the middle of nowhere?"

"Because he's white and they're black," Jules said, "and that kind of thing just didn't happen back then. Whites and blacks lived separately. Society kind of demanded it. It was so screwed up."

"So where would we find a record of who's lived in Phoenicia?" Tabby asked.

"Maybe at the library or the courts," Jules said. "I've never gone looking for anyone before. We could try both but they close at noon on Saturdays and won't be open again until Monday. Guess that means we'll have to go tubing tomorrow after all."

+++

The Gangster's Fortune

It wouldn't be fair to say the others weren't interested in finding Dutch Schultz's treasure; but they were just as interested in other things like tubing. So in the next few days, we decided to go on a tubing adventure. Jules drove us to Jessie's Tube Rental, which provided equipment for adventure seekers to experience the rapids on Esopus Creek.

Jules of course had left the house in the smallest bikini I'd ever seen and I wondered how she'd keep it on if we were going down rapids. I asked her if she was bringing another suit, just in case, and she said, "Why would I do that, Mabel?" And winked at me.

Driving there, Jules told us the course began upstream at the Jessie's headquarters, and that tubing would take about two hours. We'd get back to the car via the excursion bus.

As we were putting our lifejackets on, we were told that Esopus Creek is not a lazy river, but a class two white-water, which meant that Jules' bikini wasn't going to stay on. Still she didn't look worried. The waves would be up to three feet high and there would be rapids. Tabby said she wished she'd brought her snorkel.

The boys wore shorts and showed off their bare chests and I couldn't help looking at Hugh's scar. It had faded to brown in the sun, but it reminded me what he'd been through for me and I felt terribly guilty.

We grabbed our tubes from the huge barn full of them, and kept our trainers on, because we were told our feet might get cut on the rocks if we overturned. Wearing our life jackets and helmets, and after being asked if I was over twelve (always humiliating but nonetheless expected), we set off down the river, each on our own tube, linking arms with each other so we formed a human line across the water.

The ride started gently at first as we floated down, and then the boys started splashing us and the tubes descended into white water rapids. We separated, clinging to our tubes, and sometimes we'd wait for each other on the sides of the creek. I was thankful it was such a hot day, as the cold water was refreshing. And glad I'd kept my denim shorts on as my bum brushed against rocks on the way down.

"Isn't this exhilarating?" Tabby said, holding my hand after we'd gone through an especially active passage of water. "I like it because it's not too steep and the water can't get up your nose for more than a few seconds."

It was good to see her enjoying herself and I even let myself lie back and close my eyes a few times. It was so relaxing to drift down the river, with the sun shining on our shoulders. The boys were way ahead of us and waited for us at the end.

"Should we go down again?" Barnaby said, helping me to the side of the creek and wading into the water. He was up to his waist in the water and balanced his arms on the side of my tube.

"I told you it would be fun," Jules said. Somehow her straw hat remained perfectly placed on her blonde head. Every day was a fashion shoot in the life of Jules.

+++

The Gangster's Fortune

The next day we set off for downtown Phoenicia. Jules dropped us off at the courthouse.

"Right, and we'll meet back at the *Heron's Drift* in about an hour, outside," I said. We'd written down the information, which was only the name of a girl from the 1930s, and I wondered who might help us find out more about Desdemona and if she had anything to do with the treasure we were searching for.

The courthouse had a copper dome with the American flag flying above it. It was three stories high and grey, with pillars at the front. We walked up the steps and found a desk inside with a woman sitting behind it with a fan behind her, as it was awfully warm in the building. We told her that we were looking for information about births in the county.

She told us her name was Fiona. She asked us where we were from, as we all had accents, and said she'd always wanted to travel to England. "Head up the stairs and you'll find what you're looking for on the second floor," she said.

The Gangster's Fortune

We walked up the steps and found the records department. There we met another woman seated in front of another fan, and asked about finding out more about a child named Desdemona.

"And why would you all be looking for a child, may I ask? She's probably no relation, am I correct in thinking that?"

I nodded. "We found her diary in a shop on Main Street and we thought we might try and return it to her." It was a truthful statement. I would return the diary if we found her.

"An unusual request and unlikely that you'll find her here, but I can try. Unusual name too, she had there. We don't usually search records by first name, here. Any idea what year she might have been born in?"

"Maybe sometime in the 1920s," Tabby ventured.

She tapped long pointed red finger nails on the keys on a computer, and said it would do all the searching for her. She introduced herself, showing us her nametag that read Missy. She was a black woman with beautiful skin and her hair held up in braids.

"We're miles ahead of most other courts," she said. "We got all our records inputted into this computer about five years ago. We wanted to be able to find each other, you see. And this Desdemona, do you know any other information about her?"

"We think she lived on a track of land along Route 38," I said.

"With her mum," Tabby said.

"We can narrow searches by property as well, but we're no miracle workers here." She looked over her spectacles at us, and winked. "But I'll try my best to give you a head start to what you're looking for."

She tapped the computer a few more times. "You know, this might be your lucky day after all. There's only one Desdemona, which is hardly surprising, given her name is so unusual. Here she is. Born in 1920. She went to school here in the early part of her life, no death record though. Her school had her at this address but that would have been fifty years ago now. I'll write this down for you. At least it's worth a try to see if she's still there. Nice to see young folk exploring our great country. Now where'd you all say you was from?"

"England," Barnaby said.

"I'll betcha," she said crossing her arms in front of her chest after she'd passed the address to us.

"Desdemona Early Covington," I read.

"And no record of a marriage neither. Good luck y'all."

We walked back down the steps and back outside. I checked my watch and saw we were going to meet Hugh and Jules back at the car in ten minutes. "I hope Jules knows where this is," I said.

We sat and waited for Jules and Hugh on a bench beside the car. They took their time coming and we were hot. All of us were wearing shorts and the humidity was so high we could feel the sweat trickling down our backs.

"Where are they?" Tabby asked, getting impatient.

The Gangster's Fortune

"I can see them," Barnaby said. "They've got ice creams."

"Any luck?" I asked when they'd reached us.

"No, you?" Jules said.

I passed her the paper.

"I know where that is, not far from here, just a few blocks. Let's go see if she still lives there."

We hopped into the car and Jules carefully edged us out of the parking spot. The house was just on the edge of town but seeing that Phoenicia wasn't a very big place, we were only in the car for a few minutes when we found 1566 Larson Road.

"That's a pity," I said to the others, looking at the dilapidated farmhouse. "I can't think anyone's lived there for at least twenty years." I looked at Tabby, who was in the back seat beside me and Barnaby. There were no cars parked out front.

"I think we should go to the door and knock," she said. "Just so we know that no one's at home."

We got out of the car. Jules said she'd stay behind with the boys. Tabby and I stepped over the front stairs to the porch, as they were rotten, and made our way across the crumbling porch to the front door, which looked as if it was about to fall off its hinges. I knocked. There was no answer.

"Knock again," Tabby said, "what if there's someone dead inside?"

"Why does there always have to be someone dead inside with you, Tabby? I don't smell anything, do you?"

"Could be that they've been dead in there for years and there's just a decomposing body inside."

"May I remind you that we're not in Scotland any more or in the tunnels under Hollingsworth."

'If there was a decomposing body," Tabby prattled on, "then someone would have found it by now."

There was a mat and I bent down and pulled it back. Like the house it had seen better days. It came apart in my hand but underneath I could see a key.

"Look what I've found, Tabby! I'm going to try it."

I put the key in the lock and that was when the swing on the porch started to sway. "But there's not a breath of air, do you think there's a ghost in the swing?" Tabby said.

"I think we're going inside and we're not going to meet any ghosts or dead bodies. It's just a house, a very, very old one."

I looked over my shoulder at Hugh and Barnaby. They were sitting on the front of the car with Jules, chatting away. Hugh caught my eye and I beckoned to him to come.

The Gangster's Fortune

Chapter Eight

We stepped over the threshold and into the house, leaving the door open behind us. There was a fairly large living room and a set of stairs going up to another floor by the entrance. We walked through and near the back of the house was a kitchen. The paint was peeling off the walls and it looked as if there might have been a flood in the house years ago because the walls were slightly buckled.

"It smells so musty in here. Funny, they emptied everything out but left that."

Hugh had come in behind us. We looked where he was pointing, at an old piano in the corner. Tabby went over and put her hands on the keys and tried to play a few notes.

"They're stuck. Imagine leaving this here. It is kind of spooky, isn't it?"

"Tabby, have you got Desdemona's diary?" I asked.

"Right here," she said, taking it out of her bag.

"I'd better tell the others that there's nothing here and we'll be out in a minute," I said. I went to the door and called to Jules and Barnaby. "Nothing here, but do you want to see inside? Maybe we can all do a quick search and see what we turn up."

Tabby was reading the diary when we got back inside. "I think she's a bit older now. It's dated 1932."

I keep asking Momma about Dutch and why he hasn't come to see us for so long. She tells me to practice my letters and stop asking her questions she doesn't have the answers for. I cry at night, missing him and ask if there's a way to see him. Could we go to the city? Hush child, she says. I don't know if he's ever coming back.

I feel like I hate this house and I hate this town and I just want to move into the city and find my Poppa. It's not right that he should leave us like this. Momma's stopped her singing and cries a lot in the night and asks me to come and sleep with her.

"I wonder where her room was?" Tabby said, "Looks like there aren't any bedrooms down here. Let's look upstairs."

The five of us walked up the stairs and found three empty bedrooms. The house looked better upstairs, there were views out on to the street, but at the corner of the top of the staircase I saw that the paint was peeling. Looking up, I saw a dark yellow stain on the ceiling and wondered if there might be an attic up there too.

"Barnaby, help me get up there, would you?"

I climbed on to his shoulders and reached up until I found a small metal ring in the ceiling. I put my finger through the ring and yanked on it. A square trapdoor opened and above it there was a pull-down staircase with a rope hanging from it.

"Stand back and I'll try to pull the stairs down," Hugh said. He reached up to the rope and gave it a tug.

When the stairs came down, we stepped back and looked up. Above us was a room with wooden beams and a pitched roof.

"You first, Mabel," Tabby said.

"Coming?" I looked at her.

"There might be bats up there and I hate bats more than anything."

"I'll go up first and if there are any I'll let you know, but I'm sure everything's going to be fine."

I climbed up eight steps and entered the attic. Beneath my feet there were beams and I knew we'd be able to walk along them. The attic was quite lofty, but it smelt horribly stale. I looked along the roof and saw there was a section on the far side, near a window, where it was sagging.

Hugh came up the stairs behind me. "See anything?" he asked, poking his head through into the space.

"Not yet, looks like what you'd expect but there's something over here." I walked along the beams, hoping one foot wouldn't drop through the ceiling if the beams were rotten too. There were two small windows on either side of the attic and we could see quite well.

"Anything yet?" Tabby said, her head popping up next into the attic.

"There might be something over in this corner."

"What?"

"It looks like an old steamer trunk."

"Something you could hide money in?" she asked.

"Could be," I said, stepping closer to it.

"Anything else?"

"No, not that I can see."

I bent down over the trunk. It looked a bit like a suitcase except it had brown wooden panels all around the sides, which made it a lot deeper. The padlock on the front dangled open and I lifted the lid wondering if we might find Schultz's treasure inside. Unlikely, but certainly possible.

Instead, there were baby clothes and shoes inside, and old photos of a child, whom I presumed to be Desdemona. I felt that I oughtn't really to be looking at someone else's personal effects and wondered if I ought to stop, but I couldn't bring myself to. After all, the house was abandoned and this was just an old trunk.

It made for an interesting afternoon anyway. There were dresses in it too, dresses Desdemona's mother might have worn when she was singing in the jazz club, with rhinestones and feathered hats and heels with gold straps. It started to feel more like a dress-up trunk than anything else and I wondered why they hadn't taken it with them when they left.

Digging down deeper, I found some costume jewellery and sheets of music. That brought me to wonder about what had happened to Desdemona and her mother, and for a moment it didn't seem we were going to find anything in the trunk that might tell us anything. But then what I found was a fur coat, and I pulled it out.

"It wouldn't be wicked to want to try that on, would it?" Tabby asked.

"What are the others doing?" I asked her.

"Looking for clues in the other rooms, I dare say."

The Gangster's Fortune

Tabby put on the fur coat and rubbed the arms with her hands. "It's *so* soft. I wish I had one of these." The coat went to just above her ankles and was jet black.

"You look just like a film star," I said. "It really suits you."

"I wonder what it's made of? Do you think it's real?"

"It's probably sable or mink," said Hugh, who couldn't stand up straight to his full height in the attic.

"What do you know about furs?" I asked.

"I was going to get you one for your birthday, Mabel, but it seemed a bit over the top."

I laughed, and then we all started laughing, and I wished we were back at the beginning, when our adventures together were so much simpler and we could just do things for a lark.

"There's something in the pocket here," Tabby said. She put her hand in and pulled out a piece of paper. "What I'd do for a cigarette holder to go with this. I would look so camp. These would be props we'd have if we were doing a play."

The Gangster's Fortune

We opened the paper. It had writing scrawled across it.

I know you don't want it, but I'm giving you what I have for D. Lulu has buried it outside in the yard for me in our special place. D will know where it is.

"He must have written this on his death bed," Tabby said. "Do you think when she went to visit him she was wearing this coat, and he slipped the note into her pocket and she never noticed? It doesn't say much more than that, does it?"

Barnaby poked his head up through the opening. "Don't tell me you've actually found something? Something good?"

"Just a fur coat with what might be a letter from Schultz in the pocket, talking about something – could be the treasure - buried in the back garden here."

"Should we come up?"

"I don't want us to fall through the ceiling. We'll bring the note down to you," I said.

The Gangster's Fortune

We put the clothes back in the trunk, as neatly as we could, and then went back to the stairs, with the note, and made our way down. I showed Jules and Barnaby the note.

"It says nothing more than it was on the property then? Too bad, but at least we know that it's out there somewhere, right, whatever it is?" Jules said. She looked at the note again, and ran her finger around what looked like a scribble in the bottom corner. "This looks like a doodle to me, but what if it's a design, a picture of the place they buried the treasure?"

We all looked at the note again. The drawing was of something in the shape of a wishbone.

"One of these lines could be the creek and the other could be the highway," Jules went on, "and maybe where they meet is where they hid the treasure. Do you think we ought to go outside and take a look around? I think we ought to, to see if anything looks remotely like this symbol."

"Yes, the sooner we get out of the house the better," Barnaby said, "especially since we're not really supposed to be in here anyway, are we?

Mind you, the garden won't be any better. It's still someone else's property."

"You can stay in the car if you like," Hugh replied, "but we're going around the back."

After the boys pushed the staircase back up into the ceiling, we hurried down the stairs and out of the front door. I put the key back under the mat, and that was when I heard the sound of a rifle being cocked behind my head.

"You all moving into this old farm house?"

I turned and saw a man on the front lawn with his rifle pointed at us. "I never saw a "For Sale" sign. Something you want to tell me?"

We looked at each other, unsure what we should say.

"We're from England and we're researching the Dutch Schultz story," I said, looking at Barnaby.

"So you thought you'd just mosey on inside, did you? I ought to call the cops. Where are your parents?"

"That's not necessary, is it?" Jules said.

"And who might you be? You sound like you're from here."

The Gangster's Fortune

"That's because I am. My family has a place on Wappinger Creek. I'm Darla's girl."

"Darla? I knew her when she was about this big." He lowered his hand until it was near his hip. "Why didn't you just say so? I'm Cliff, and I'm sorry about the gun, but you can't be too careful with strangers around here. Don't none of you have a notebook, if you're doing research?"

Barnaby looked relieved now that the gun was pointed at the ground. "We've had a look at the areas around Phoenicia. We'll probably have a film crew with us, next time you see us. We're with the BBC."

"The BBC?"

"The British Broadcast Corporation."

"All of you?"

Barnaby nodded.

"Ah ha. You'd best be off then, and say hi to Darla next time you see her."

He wandered off down the street and a few doors later went into a house.

"Have all Americans got guns?" I asked.

The Gangster's Fortune

Jules nodded. "It's part of our Constitution's Second Amendment rights. We have the right to keep and bear arms. In most places you don't even need a permit or registration documents. You can just go to a store and get one like a jug of milk."

"Have you got one, Jules?" Barnaby asked.

"No, I don't, but people want the right. It's important to them. It's a big part of being American. Not something that makes sense at all to me. Let's get in the car and go home. My mother would kill me if they called the cops on us. We're going to have to find another way to get to the back of the property, as coming up to the front door is too obvious."

"Who's Darla, by the way?" I asked as we pulled out.

"My mom. It's the name she had before she moved into the city and became Vivian. He'd never be able to find her now, though."

"Here," she said as she passed the note to me.

I stared at the wishbone, wondering what it meant, and if it had anything to do with Dutch

The Gangster's Fortune

Schultz's treasure. And how we would get past Cliff if we were to come back.

"We could sneak on to the property off the highway," Jules said. "If we pulled on to one of the back lanes, no one would see us."

"This is mad," Barnaby said. "We've just had someone point their gun at us. Doesn't that bother any of you in the slightest? Because it does me, and that story about preliminary research, I had to make that up, and it meant lying through my teeth."

"It's a good thing you did, though," Hugh said, "but I have to say your sister's even braver than you are. Maybe you're not cut out for treasure hunting after all."

It sounded cruel, but Hugh was right. Neither of them liked being in danger very much and I felt guilty for going into the house in the first place. But we had found the note, so now we knew where we had to look. All in all, it had been worth it.

+++

The Gangster's Fortune

We went down to the local grocery shop to buy some food, enough to last us a few days at least, each of us chipping in some cash, and then we drove back to the cottage for a cup of tea.

As it was out of the sun, the house was cool inside, and so we went to our rooms to change into lighter clothes.

"Now what?" Barnaby said, coming into the kitchen and putting his arms around my waist from behind.

"Thank you for talking Cliff down, he seemed to believe you."

"Hugh's right, maybe I don't have the stomach for this." He kissed my neck.

I turned around to face him and put my arms around his neck. I wanted to stay like that.

"You did fine. But if you want to stay here next time we go, that'll be fine too."

"Don't tell me you're thinking of going back?" Barnaby let me go.

"Of course we'll be going back. I know it got a little bit frightening, but it was fun just the same, finding things that haven't been touched for years,

The Gangster's Fortune

and then wondering what they might mean and what would be the right thing to do with them. I know it can be a bit much at the start, but really it's great fun."

Barnaby gave me a look, let me go and crossed his arms in front of his chest. "You didn't even flinch when the gun was pointed at you, Mabel. How come?"

"It's not the first time someone's pointed a gun at me, you know."

That was when Jules came in and told us she was going to call her mum. She picked up the wall phone that was hanging beside the cabinets. It had a long cord so you could practically walk around the living room with it.

"Hi Mom, it's me. We just met an old friend of yours, someone called Cliff. Do you remember him? Yes, he said to say hello to you. Yes, we're fine. Talk to you later. And yes, the car is fine too. Thanks for letting us use the house. We went tubing and it was the best. Everyone's great. Bye."

Jules went to look in the drawers of the desk in the living room and came back with a map of the area and a sheet with symbols on it. She'd changed back into her bikini top and short shorts. Barnaby was finding it pretty hard to keep his eyes off her.

"What if this symbol is something like the hobo code?"

We stared at her, not knowing what she meant.

She smiled, and went on to explain. "You know, during the Depression back in the 1930s there were so many homeless men who went travelling around the country on the railroads, and they used to leave signs like this around, sort of a language because they may not have been able to read and write, so they'd draw symbols on fences to warn other guys like them of what might be inside a house if they knocked on the door. My mom used to be into learning about this stuff, and she showed me this sheet years ago."

We scanned it. "No wishbones here," Tabby said.

"But Dutch Schultz never was a hobo, was he?" I asked. "Let's read some more from Desdemona's diary."

The Gangster's Fortune

"Barnaby got me some beer at the store. You're welcome to have one if you like." Jules pulled a six pack out of the fridge. "There's at least one for everyone."

"Thanks, Jules," Hugh said, twisting off the cap. "Cold beer tastes good on a hot day."

Not exactly my cup of tea, and not Tabby's either.

"More for us, then," Jules said. She seemed disappointed.

"1932," Tabby read, "so that's about three years before his actual death, Dutch, I mean."

"Go on then," Hugh looked over at her.

I've just turned 11 years old and Dutch gave Momma a new fur coat which she wears around the house and calls herself an African Queen. I say I must be an African Princess and she smiles. We have bacon for breakfast that Dutch has brought us from the city and it tastes like heaven. I want him to stay with us all the time but Momma says he's too busy with his business and we should be grateful for the time we have with him. But I want more. For my birthday he said he was giving me a special surprise but I don't know what it is yet. He's coming back on Sunday and said he'll bring it with him. I can't wait.

It's Sunday now and Dutch brought me more dolls than I can count. I've given them all names and I put them to bed with me every night. We like to go walking around in the woods behind the house and we found a special spot.

"You're not going to believe this," Tabby said. "There's a picture of that wishbone here." We all gathered around behind her.

"Keep reading, don't keep us in suspense," Jules urged her, perched right on the edge of her seat. "We just might find something." She looked at Barnaby and even he seemed interested.

We've made a trail in the woods, we walk so far back that we can't see the house and I feel like we are in another country, maybe even another time, and with Dutch holding my hand I can only

The Gangster's Fortune

say that he is the best Poppa I could ever have, even though he won't let me call him that.

We walked and he let me wear his hat, which he never does. It's white with a black band and made of something like straw. He calls it a Fedora and says it gives him special powers. Like what? I asked him. And he smiled at me, and said to find things, people like you and your Momma and when he wears it he says nothing can ever hurt him.

When I asked why someone would want to hurt him, he patted the top of my head and said that one day I'd read about him but I mustn't believe all the things they write because only half of them is true.

We found a place, a special place, and he asked me if I knew what a wishbone looked like because he said the trees we were looking at were planted in the shape of a wishbone. I asked him if he meant the wishbone from a chicken that Momma and I made wishes on and pulled apart for good luck and he chuckled.

He took me out to the edge of the pine trees and we looked back at them, and he asked me if I could see that the trees looked like they was planted like the end of a wishbone with a few at the top and then lines of trees going in a line to the left and the right.

I wasn't sure what he meant so he drew in my book and showed me the symbol and said the end of the wishbone was where all the luck in the world happened. At least that's what his Momma had told him about wishbones.

And he stood on the spot just behind the tree at the furthest tip of the wishbone and said that this was the spot he'd come to think about things, to keep things, that's what he said, and he took me in his arms and held me close and I hugged his neck as tight as I could. He said he wanted us to stay this way for always but I had to forgive him if things changed.

1936

I had no idea how much things could change. Dutch is dead. Gunned down and then they came for Momma and she went to the attic while the men was banging on the door in her fur coat and when

The Gangster's Fortune

she came back she wasn't wearing the coat and said it was over and I should go and hide out under my bed. And I did and then I heard the shotgun and the men marched into my room and looked around and to each other said "there was a kid, here kiddie kiddie," like I was some kind of cat.

But I was too afraid to come out. One of them told the other to leave me be and then they left and I ran out to Momma. She was on the floor with blood all around her and she said to call her sister Frannie, and I held her on the floor and remembered how she'd told me to call the police if anything bad ever happened, and this was bad, the worst thing that had ever happened to me, so I went and called the police and they came and took Momma away because they told me she was dead.

And put a blanket over her face, but I didn't want to leave her so I ran behind the stretcher and wailed and this woman put in me in the back of the police car and took me down to the police station and they called someone about me.

And they brought me to this foster home in Phoenicia and I guess I'll never get to go and see that grove of trees again, or Dutch or Momma, and I'll never get to be no-one.

"That's the saddest thing I've ever heard," Tabby said.

"We could check and see if she's in the foster system. I wonder if we could find her now," I felt sad too.

"I wonder if she's still alive," Hugh said.

"Wouldn't it be neat to find her? I mean if we found the treasure." Tabby said. "Then it would all be hers. Especially since we have the diary to prove who her father was."

"You might need more than that diary to prove Dutch Schultz was her father, but we can try," Jules said. "We have to go and see about those trees and maybe it will be right there waiting for us. The treasure, that is."

"Jules and I were talking," Barnaby said, as we all sat in front of the TV trying to relax. "And there's a walk we'd like to go on that goes up to an old hotel called the Overlook. Maybe it would do us all good to take a break from the treasure hunting, just for a day or so." He still looked scared. A day off would do him good.

We all agreed but I wished we didn't. I wanted to find the treasure before something happened and no one else seemed to want to believe that we needed to hurry.

Chapter Nine

The next day Jules drove us deep into the Catskills. It was near the end of July and Jules said this was the hottest time of the year in this part of the country. She told us that the first Overlook hotel had been a small lodge, built by a developer in 1833. Business had never taken off, though, and a new developer had tried again in 1871 with a 300-room hotel on the site, but that hotel had burned down in 1875, and the rebuild burned down in 1921.

"So what's left of it?" Tabby asked.

"I guess we'll see soon enough," Jules said as she pulled the car into a place where the trail head started. We got out and walked down a gravel road which would take us to the top of Overlook Mountain.

"It's an easy ten-mile hike," Jules said. "And we'll see the old ruins at about two miles along."

We walked here and there behind Jules, Hugh beside me and Barnaby beside his sister.

The Gangster's Fortune

When we reached the old ruins they looked like something haunted, something stripped down to its concrete bones. It stood two stories above us, amongst the trees, reclaimed from man by nature. A skeleton amongst the green of trees and branches.

"We should walk on," Jules said, "just ahead there's an old fire tower. We can walk to the top."

When we came to the tower it looked like something that the wind might blow over. There were many steps leading up to a box-like structure on the top of what looked like an antenna tower. As we climbed the stairs and got to the top, Jules pointed out the Hudson River and the Ashokan Reservoir, the Westkill Mountains and Overlook Mountain. She told us the last time she'd come as a girl with her brothers they'd seen a rattlesnake and she had been so terrified they had to carry her back down on their shoulders, all the way down.

She led us up to Echo Lake, where we had our picnic and looked out. It had taken us three hours to reach the lake and we were happy just to sit. Jules and Barnaby went for a swim after telling us they deserved a dip after climbing 1300 feet, and they raced each other across to the other side of the lake. Tabby went for a stroll around the lake leaving Hugh and me alone.

"It's my favourite bit of coming on these trips with you, Mabel," he said. "I know you like the treasure, and so do I, but I love just seeing a place, and getting to know it." He pulled his sketch pad out of his bag and started to look around.

I stared at him, his blonde curly hair falling over his face, his shirt on the rock beside him. I couldn't stop looking at the scar.

"It was worth it, if you're wondering, that is."

"Wondering what?"

"If getting stabbed was worth getting you to safety. Knowing you'd be all right, knowing that you wouldn't be taken away from me."

"Does it hurt?"

"No, just my shoulder, sometimes it aches."

"And you must wish you'd never met me." I looked at his face. And then at the pad of paper. He was sketching me sitting next to him.

The Gangster's Fortune

"You know, I never get tired of your face, Mabel, trying to get the likeness right. I can't explain to anyone what it is about you, why I'd give my life again if I had to, to protect you, I just would."

"You should never have been put in that position. We should have gone home when we got the card at the Dead Sea."

"But you found all that treasure, Mabel."

"But I lost you, the most important thing of all."

He looked at me, his fingers clasping the pencil, making rough strokes with it and rubbing parts of them to smudge the pencil lines on the paper.

"I shouldn't have walked away last autumn," he said. "I shouldn't have done that to you. I know that now. I was so unhappy. So miserable and I couldn't reach out to you. I wanted to so much. I wanted you to know that in my heart I never left you. I never stopped sketching you. I never stopped wondering if you still felt the same way, if you wanted to change things and make them the way they were before. I wanted to know if you still loved me Mabel. Do you?"

I couldn't look at him.

Barnaby came running out of the water and ran towards me, unaware of the conversation. He picked me up from the rock and charged back into the water with me.

"No," I shouted. "No!"

Then he threw me up in the air and I plunged into the lake. When I surfaced, Hugh had gone, with his bag and his sketchbook.

I played in the water with Jules and Barnaby, thinking about what Hugh had said, knowing I would never be able to put him at risk like that again.

+++

Next morning, we filled up the boot of Jules's Jaguar with shovels and spades, taking a few maps from the bookshelves in the house as well as Desdemona's diary, with its description of the trees in the shape of a wishbone.

The Gangster's Fortune

We packed sandwiches and crisps and a thermos of iced tea, and piled into the car. On one of the maps Jules had found a back road that led to the farmhouse property and we set out, confident we would find what had been hidden all those years ago.

Everyone had questions about what we'd do when we found the treasure, if we'd call the police first or our parents, and we all decided we should call the police and maybe even drive the treasure down to the police station ourselves. The mood was a bit frenzied though, with everyone laying down the law and telling everyone else when they thought we'd find the treasure and who the actual person to do so would be.

When we reached the turn-off, Jules slowed the car down and drove along at a crawl so as not to attract any attention. But really, we were driving a Jaguar and I wondered how many of them there were in Phoenicia.

Jules stopped the car at the far end of the lane, out of sight of the highway and hidden from the road, which was probably a mile away from where the farmhouse stood. We could see it in the distance, so I thought we'd best try to walk across the piece of land to see if we could find the spot where the treasure was buried.

"Should we bring a spade?" Hugh asked.

"Maybe we should leave everything here for now and come back for it later." I didn't fancy having to answer questions about picks and shovels when we could easily say we'd been out for a walk and had somehow got on to the wrong piece of land.

"Let's leave it all," I said.

Barnaby took my hand as we started down the scree to the land and then helped me over the barbed wire fence. The others went over and under it to avoid getting caught on it.

Jules had her map of the area and had marked off where she thought the property lines might be, so we set off towards the morning sun, not realizing just how big the piece of land was or how much ground we'd have to cover.

"My brothers kept these walkie-talkies out in the shed and they still work. I think we should fan

The Gangster's Fortune

out in groups. I've made a copy for you Mabel, we'll check in and keep track of each other so we're not all stomping over the same area and going round and round in circles. I think each group should have one of the boys."

"I'll go with Mabel, shall I?" Barnaby said.

"And I'll come too," Tabby said.

"We'll check in with the walkie-talkies every twenty minutes, sound good?" Jules asked.

I looked at the map Jules had drawn for us, with its grid pattern and quadrants, to make sure we covered the whole piece of land.

"See you later, then." I looked at Hugh and Jules.

"First one to the trees, let the other group know which grid you're in," Jules said, "and we'll meet there."

We trudged off to the north-east side of the plot and Jules and Hugh to the north-west. The ground was more treed than I'd expected and it felt like we were walking in a forest.

I thought it unlikely we'd find a ring of trees but it didn't seem worth mentioning that to the others. We walked, passing the thermos of iced tea between us, and talked about the size of the plot. It rose up sharply beside us, so we kept to the bottom of the hills, fanning out to cover the most ground.

"Not seeing anything but trees here," Tabby said into the walkie-talkie. "What if someone came and cut them all down and these are new growth? I mean they were here in the 1930s, that's fifty years ago, these were probably just little baby trees then." She sounded discouraged.

It occurred to me that the piece of land was so big – two football pitches long and perhaps as wide as three – that it was no wonder that no one had ever found this treasure. To think that we could just walk among the trees and find it on our first try was pretty close to impossible.

As the morning stretched into afternoon and we'd found nothing and neither had the others, we met back at the car for lunch. Barnaby looked relieved.

"Let's come back tomorrow," I said. "We can't expect to find it on the first day, can we? And maybe we'll have better luck closer to the house."

The Gangster's Fortune

"I may be out of line here," Jules said, "but I did want to take you up to a waterfall for a hike tomorrow. Couldn't this wait at least a few days? It's so depressing not finding anything and just trudging around in the hot sun. Shall we vote?"

And, of course, they all voted against me wanting to return in the morning.

That was to be expected and it didn't bear mentioning that the longer we took finding the treasure the more we put ourselves at risk. They seemed content that not hearing from my mother meant that she really was locked away for good, and I seemed to be the only one giving it a second thought.

+++

The next day, Jules drove us and told us it was only a short hike in and would take less than an hour. Barnaby and I set out ahead on the trail and a little while later we found the falls. They looked about fifteen feet high. When the others had joined us, we hiked up to a ledge behind the lower falls and felt the mist rising up from the pool below.

The Gangster's Fortune

It was so beautiful and unspoiled that we stood and watched, transfixed by the water coming down. Tabby and the boys continued to hike up and found spots where they could cliff jump into the water below. That wasn't my sort of thing at all. Instead, I hiked down and sat watching the others, thinking how happy they sounded and what a lovely way this was to spend the day.

Jules had got talking to some other hikers she'd met on the path and I saw them exchanging numbers before she came and joined me. "They're from San Francisco," she said, "but here in the state for the summer too. Never hurts to make new friends. So how are you, Mabel? I feel like we haven't had much time to talk about anything since you've been here."

I started to wade into the water and Jules followed me.

"I've been worrying about Harris, my birth father. I know he's coming and the longer we take to find the treasure the more time he has."

"To what?"

"To hurt us."

The Gangster's Fortune

"I get that you're worried, but you weren't really going to come all this way and not have any fun, were you?" Jules asked.

"What about your dad, Jules, your real dad? Where's he now?"

I felt like we'd come all this way but I didn't know her any better than I had in Petra.

"Dad's complicated," she said. "He had a drinking problem, and Mom basically said he had to quit or leave. And I guess he liked the bottle more than he liked us. We were living here then, I was little, and I don't remember much of him, except that he loved working on cars in our garage, where I could usually find him drinking. They got into a nasty fight one day, and he ended up smashing a bunch of our stuff and Mom told him to go."

"What was he like before the drinking?" I asked.

"He was sweet. You know, never shaved, never changed his clothes much at all, so you can see why Mom wanted him out. He didn't have any drive. Couldn't keep a job. Was a bum, really."

"What was his name?"

The Gangster's Fortune

"Monty Pesever. He liked to take me to the gun range."

"So you can shoot?"

"In a pinch. Not well, but I know a little about guns. He just wasn't a great guy. A terrible husband and not too good on the father side of things either. He was just stuck being somewhere he didn't want to be so he left and we haven't heard a word from him since. It's hard when someone that's supposed to love you doesn't care a thing about you."

"I'm sorry," I said.

"No need to be, we all have our stuff, don't we? Things that we wish we could change. People in our lives we wish we could change. It would be so easy if we could all start over. If there were no messy bits. Is it like that with you and Hugh?"

"Yes, I suppose it is."

"Too late to go back now?"

"Are you fishing?" I asked not sure if she was being serious or not. "I don't know, Jules. It makes me sad to think about it being over forever."

"Forever is a long time. Some things just aren't meant to work out so other things can.

The Gangster's Fortune

They're not meant to be and it's best to just let them go." She looked sad.

"Are you remembering your dad?"

"A little. But only for a minute. He doesn't deserve more than that."

Then she started to splash me. I ran towards her, splashing her back until she dived under to escape. I looked up to see Hugh jumping off one of the cliffs above me. He plunged in and then surfaced. "I thought I saw you down here. Fresh, isn't it?" he said, swimming over to me.

"Do you think I don't care about having fun?" I asked him.

"You're here, aren't you?"

We swam over underneath the waterfall, and sat on a shelf behind it, watching the others jumping down from above.

"You wouldn't have found all the treasures you have if you liked watching telly more than going outside, would you? And those were good things you did. You've lived more in the past seventeen years than most people do in a lifetime. Nothing scares you. I worry about that sometimes. I worry about you. And I worry that we may never have another day like this," he said taking my hand. "Where we can just be free together." He kissed it.

"Like when we used to help Alim in Jordan with collecting the firewood and putting it on the donkey. We were free then as we are now to explore the world. To make memories and to be together."

"What did you mean when you said you're worried we won't have another day like this?" I asked.

"I mean that time is slipping away. Soon we'll go off to school, and make different friends and I suppose we'll grow up. And we'll never be here, at the point again."

"It's too soon to know that. We have so much living to do."

"But Mabel, you live your life on the edge. I worry that you'll drop off one day. That you'll get lost in the need to find your mother and bring her to justice."

"Hugh, she's already in prison. I saw her for myself."

The Gangster's Fortune

"I just think she'll always haunt you. And I worry about that. I worry that she'll take your life from you and you'll wake up one day and look back on this day, these days, and think that you wished you'd had more of them."

"I do want more days like this." I looked at Hugh. "With you. And when we get home I'll have had enough. I'll be a normal teenager."

Hugh laughed. "You're cold in the shade here." He rubbed my arm. "Your teeth are even chattering."

"Kiss me," I said. "As if this is the last time you will."

He put his hand up to my cheek and put his lips on mine and pulled me in close and I could feel his breath on my lips, "Mabel," he said, "you'll always be mine."

Chapter Ten

Next day, we set off for the land behind the farmhouse again, this time taking the spades and shovels from the back of the Jaguar.

"I suggest we do a final sweep back towards the house," Tabby said. "Desdemona was just a little girl when she wrote her diary, so perhaps it isn't that far to the spot she was talking about. I think it would be better, too, if we all went together, if that's all right with everyone, because that way we could get back home around four."

I felt so grateful that she and the others wanted to spend the day searching, and so off we went.

We set out towards the house, and the forest was still thick. After about forty-five minutes, however, the trees started to thin out and we came to a spot that looked as if it might have been a clearing in the past. At some point, a number of pine trees had been planted here, and they stood out so clearly from among the other trees because they were so much taller.

I stepped back and said to the others, "I think this is the place. Look at the trees. See how the largest ones are growing in two lines, one down each side. This must be the place Desdemona was talking about in her diary. She said it was near the tree at the top of the arc of the wishbone."

We all looked at the trees and saw that they had been planted in a pattern that was already familiar to us, on paper, at least. We took sips from our thermoses and then looked around for a tree or a rock with a carving on it, but found nothing. It seemed that any sign or symbol that might have been left behind had been washed away by the erosion of time.

I turned around, looking for Hugh, hoping he might have something to offer. He was sitting on the ground, drinking his coffee, and when I leant over to ask him, something caught my eye. On the tree behind him, only a foot or so off the ground, was a carving, a heart shape with the letters D+D in the centre. It was so faint that if I hadn't been down almost on my knees, I would have missed it altogether, and I realized in a flash that it had been carved that low so that only a child could see it.

"Look what's there," I gasped, pointing at the carving so the others would see it. "You know, I think we've found the right spot. Let's try digging here, right in front of this tree."

We had nothing else to go on, so it seemed like a good idea. We got the shovels and spades, and took turns at digging until we were all dripping with sweat and almost ready to give up. Then, about four feet down, the boys hit on something hard.

"It's probably just a big stone," Hugh said, "but there again, it might be something else. Mabel, would you and the girls get the spades, please, and dig the soil away from around where I hit so we can find out what really is down there?"

We dug around the hard spot, clearing the soil away, and as the hole got wider and deeper we saw that it wasn't a rock at all but something that looked like a body bag.

The Gangster's Fortune

"Oh no, that's horrible." Tabby stood up. "It's a dead body. Who knows how many people he buried in here. This could well be a grave, not a hiding place for treasure." She looked as if she was about to cry.

"Keep digging, Mabel," Hugh said, seeing that Tabby had just about given up.

Jules wasn't so put off and she and I went on digging until we managed to clean out all the corners around the bag, when it became clear that something else was wrapped in it, something large and square, not a body after all. We found the opening and pulled it back. Inside were two identical suitcases, one on top of the other.

"I thought he'd buried a safe. That would have been much harder to get into the car." Tabby looked relieved.

"I think we should try and get them open first," I said. "There's no point in taking them anywhere if they're just filled with dolls or comics or something a little girl hid."

"Five feet down?" Barnaby said. "She could never have dug a hole this deep on her own. This would have taken men to do."

He was right. Looking at them, it was pretty obvious that a little girl would never have been able wrap two suitcases in a body bag and then bury them in the ground, but we still couldn't be sure what was in them until we opened them.

Barnaby looked at Tabby. "Would you give me a hand with the straps, please?" He asked.

We knelt in the hole. The handles on the suitcases had rotted away, making them look more like briefcases or something a travelling medicine man might have kept all his samples in. On the side of each case were gold corners and snap locks that you could open by pressing on the tabs beside them. I pushed on the tabs but the locks remained closed.

"Does anyone have a hammer or an axe?" Now I felt like the one who was about to perform some disturbing act.

The Gangster's Fortune

Barnaby looked in the tool bag we had also brought with us. "There's one here," he said, and handed me a hammer.

I took it and, swinging it as hard as I could, hit each tab on the top suitcase until it sprung open. Then I lifted the lid. Inside, the first thing I saw were green American dollar bills, stacks and stacks of them. Underneath them were what looked like bonds, and underneath those were a number of gold bars, like the ones you see in a bank vault on television, all stacked up one on top of the other. I wasn't strong enough to lift the case out myself, so Tabby, Jules and I lifted it up to Hugh and then we all climbed out.

"Why don't we open the other one now, Mabel?" Tabby said.

Hugh jumped down into the hole and lifted the suitcase up to Barnaby, who hammered on the tabs just as I had, and when we took the top off, inside we found more stacks of dollar bills on one side of the case and on the other side a pouch with a drawstring.

The Gangster's Fortune

I took out the pouch, pulled on the string and felt inside it. "I think they're jewels, maybe diamonds," I said, taking out a handful and pouring them into a little mound on the palm of my other hand. "Gosh, there's lots of them. Wow, there was never any mention of diamonds in what we read."

The others were as transfixed as I was by the sparkling stones.

"Why not just put them back in the pouch," Tabby said, "in case you sneeze or something, and they scatter all over the place." She always was the practical one, Tabby.

I put them back in the pouch and then put it back into the suitcase.

"We did it," I said, feeling a glow.

"I never would have believed you'd do it again, Mabel," Hugh said, beaming with pride.

"Should we fill the hole up again?" Barnaby asked.

"No, the police will want to see where we found it, won't they?" Tabby said.

"Well done, Mabel," said a voice coming from another direction.

The Gangster's Fortune

My heart sank. I turned and looked. Coming out of the trees with a pistol in his hand was my birth father, Harris Walker. He was wearing jeans and a faded blue linen shirt, and his hair was longer now, curly like mine. And the pistol had a silencer on it. "We need to go back to the house, Mabel," he said, "and in short order, too."

"We're not going anywhere with you," Barnaby said. "Who do you think you are?

"You'll go where I tell you to. I'm Mabel's father. Her natural father. Maybe she didn't want to tell you about me. But he knows who I am." He gestured in the direction of Hugh. "I still can't believe you survived. It's a miracle really. It took a lot for you to jump into the helicopter and save Mabel. But I gather things have been a touch difficult between you two since then. As expected. That was the point really."

I stared at Harris, wondering how on earth he'd managed to find us, and how we were going to get the better of him.

"I've been keeping my eye on you, Mabel. We had some bugs put in the cottage and at the flat, so we knew everything you were thinking almost before you thought it. Pity you weren't a bit more thorough in your search of the premises and that no one else seemed in the slightest worried by the notion of us coming for you. They assumed that just because your mother's in prison she couldn't reach you. Silly, silly children. Down on your knees now, and hands behind your backs."

"I'll come with you, just let my friends go," I yelled at him.

"No need to shout, Mabel, no one can hear you out here. We've got plans and the future depends on you cooperating."

"I will never cooperate with you or my mother," I spat at him.

"Just as I thought." He raised the gun and shot Barnaby in the side, just above his waist.

"Barnaby!" Tabby screamed racing over to him. Barnaby slumped down and fell forward in the grass. Tabby pulled him back so he was lying between her legs. She started crying and telling him it would be all right.

The Gangster's Fortune

"Why'd you do that? He's never done anything to you!" I screamed at Harris, running over to him. "I hate you. I hate you with all my heart and I will never, ever want you to be part of my life." I tried to push him over, but he slapped me across the face with his hand and I fell down again.

"I need you to know that I mean what I say." He pointed the gun at my head. "The others will be next if you don't listen. Hugh, pick him up and carry him back to the house now, and if I hear so much as a whisper of one of you trying to make a run for it, I'll shoot him again, and this time I won't miss his heart. No one really likes a bloodbath now, do they? And besides, I've got special instructions on what I'm to do with you."

"Who are the instructions from?" I asked.

"You breathe another word, Mabel and I'll kill them both." He looked over at Hugh, who was lifting Barnaby up as gently as he could, and with Tabby's help getting him on to his back. I didn't doubt him for a second.

At that moment another man stepped out of the forest, a hulking great figure, perhaps six-foot-six tall and thick in build, with a shiny suit and a bald head. His had silver chains on his wrists and large square glasses and a black turtleneck that didn't quite come up to his Adam's apple. I felt my stomach heave.

"This is Benny," Harris said. "One of our... acquaintances."

"If you knew where the treasure was, then why didn't you just come and get it yourself?" I muttered under my breath, frightened that any slip on my part now would mean more pain for my friends.

"Where would the fun in that be? And besides, we didn't know the exact spot, so we had to follow you in, just parked on the highway. You were none the wiser. We'll take the bags though. You have to give them to us. You pass them to Benny, Tabitha."

I looked away from him and realized that I couldn't see Jules anywhere. I didn't say a word, just hoped that she might have stolen away from us and managed to get to the car. Harris marched us all back in the direction of the house.

The Gangster's Fortune

"Where's Jules?" he said to me.

"She felt sick and had to go back to the city. She's coming back tomorrow."

"You are almost as good at lying as your mother. It's so rude of you not even to take the time to introduce me to your new friend."

Blood was bubbling out of Barnaby's mouth and running down Hugh's back.

Harris ducked behind Hugh and grabbed a handful of Barnaby's hair. "How did she convince you both to come?" he snarled. "Her mother's like that, so persuasive. What a pity you decided to join her."

We were getting close to the farmhouse. Harris was walking behind me now and I could feel the back of his gun pressing against the nape of my neck.

"Go round the front, Benny, put the bags in the boot, and be sure you lock it."

Benny disappeared with the suitcases. He had one under each arm, because they wouldn't close again.

The Gangster's Fortune

"We've been doing a bit of renovating," Harris said.

We could see they'd put boards up on all the windows to black them out. He had us walk up the back steps, through the kitchen and into the living room.

"Get down on the floor and stay there."

Hugh lowered Barnaby gently on the floor and crouched down beside him. He was losing a lot of blood. Harris went over to them, with a furious look on his face like he'd been seized by some fit of jealous rage. He grabbed Barnaby's hair again and blood rolled out of the side of Barnaby's mouth. Harris didn't even seem to notice.

"What you been doing to my little girl, eh?"

Barnaby's eyes blinked open and his hand clutched his side. "Nothing. Nothing at all," he whispered.

"You have such an honest face, just like your sister, I almost believe you. Well, now I'm going to light a fire."

The words filled me with dread. What did he mean to do to us?

The Gangster's Fortune

Benny was back in minutes, looking for advice as to what to do next. Harris pointed at the petrol cans at the foot of the stairs. "Slosh the petrol up and down the stairs. Be generous with it."

We watched in horror as Benny grabbed three cans in each hand and began to shake the petrol up the walls, and down on the floor. We heard him walk upstairs.

"You're going to set the house on fire?" I said. "Why?"

"Because your friends are going to be in it. It's time to leave your childhood behind, Mabel. Your mother doesn't want you to have any more distractions." He nodded at the others. "You're all going to die, here and now."

"When I visited her in prison," I interrupted him, "she said that someone else had taken me and left me on the steps of the church. Who was it that took me away from Grace, Harris?"

Harris's demeanour changed. He put a hand behind his neck and cracked it. "He did. He took you from us. We wanted you. Always have. Never wanted you to be called Mabel, though. And he locked your mum up like she was some sort of animal. I suppose she didn't tell you that much."

"Locked her up where?"

"It doesn't matter now. She kept all the things she'd made for you and hid them in a locker at the swimming pool, where she thought he'd never find them. But I knew they were there."

"What was in the locker?" I asked.

"The usual sort of things she collected for when you'd come." He was walking around the circle now, the circle we'd formed. "She never made it to the hospital, you see. He wouldn't let her go there, so there were no hospital armbands. We never got to see you with all the other babies, in a row, like you see in the films. But she never gave up. She just bided her time and said when you became a young woman you'd be ready to join us. We never counted on these three, though."

"Didn't she realize I'm the daughter of a policeman?" I asked.

"You think that would stop her? She's obsessed with you and anyone you love. That's why you should say your goodbyes now."

The Gangster's Fortune

Tabby started to cry.

"If all goes well, you'll be burned to a crisp. Ashes to ashes, dust to dust, and all that."

"And what about my parents? Are you going to kill them too?" I asked.

"Kill? Such a strong word. No: they'll be in an accident as soon as Grace is out for good conduct, and that shouldn't be much more than a few weeks now, after the bribes have gone through, and I'm supposed to bring you straight to her, Mabel. That's the way she wants it. Pity about your American friend, but she'll come soon enough, I'm betting on that."

Where was Jules? Why hadn't she come to save us? Had she gone to find Cliff the neighbour, and he wasn't home? I feared for the worst. We were quite possibly all going to die here, if Barnaby wasn't close enough to it already. Everything was going to go up as soon as Harris struck a match.

"All set, boss," Benny said when he came back.

"I'm taking them up to the attic. Up the stairs, now!" he ordered, and looking over at Benny he said, "you take Mabel and lock her in the car. She's coming with us. Do anything you need to, to keep her quiet, but remember, she's got to come back to England alive and ready to work, so no maiming this time."

I wondered if Benny even knew what that meant.

Benny grabbed me by the arm. "I hear you can be a right handful."

He pulled a knife out of his pocket. "I like knives and I like putting them to use. What a disappointment you're so precious." Then he dragged me out of the back door and down beside the house until we came to a car that was parked on the road in front. I didn't recognize it; it wasn't like the van they'd used to spy on us in Scotland. We came round to the front of the car.

"You say a thing and I'll carve your face, little girl."

He turned to unlock the car door and reached over to open it.

Suddenly, out of the corner of my eye, I saw Jules running towards us with a spade, its metal

The Gangster's Fortune

blade held high over her head. She brought it down on Benny's head and hit him with it again and again until he dropped to the ground.

"You're not going anywhere, Mabel Hartley," she said. "I popped the hood and cut a bunch of wires. The car's toast. Let them try to get away with the treasure this time."

"Oh Jules, I've never been happier to see anyone in my whole life. You've saved me, thank you! But it's not over, we need to keep him out for the count."

We were on the front lawn of the old dilapidated farmhouse, two teenagers, and no one had come out of their houses to see if they could help.

"There's some bleach back here, looks like a bit of blood too," Jules looked through the back windows of the car. "Probably for cleaning upholstery after they've knocked someone off. Do you know who these people are, Mabel?"

"One of them is my father, Harris. The other one looks like a mob fellow. They're bad news. You wouldn't have any nail polish remover in your bag,

Jules, would you?" I asked, terrified that Benny might regain consciousness any second.

She smiled and went to get the bleach, and then took the nail polish remover from her bag. "What are you going to do with these?"

"Together these agents work like chloroform. Should keep him out for a while."

She took off her sweater and passed it to me. "Use this."

I doused her sweater until it was nice and wet and then held it over his nose and mouth. "We won't be able to lift him so we'd better tie his hands behind his back." I reached into my rucksack and found the handcuffs I liked to keep in there for emergencies.

"Now you stay here and call the police and don't under any circumstance let Benny out of your sight. Scream for help if you have to and hit him with the shovel again. I'm going in to help the others. We don't have a lot of time."

"Where are they?"

The Gangster's Fortune

"I think Harris is taking them to the attic. He got Benny to pour petrol everywhere, so I'm expecting him to light a match any second."

"Please be careful," Jules hugged me and I wondered if we'd ever see each other again. "You've been such a great friend, Jules." I was crying now.

"Stop talking like this is over. You're Mabel Hartley and you're going to go in there and save them all because you are the bravest girl I know."

I wiped my cheeks with the sleeves of my arms.

"What if they all die?"

"They will if you don't get going. You can do it."

"Thanks, Jules, stay safe." I hugged her again.

Flames were starting to shoot out of the downstairs windows. I wanted to run as fast and as far as I could away from there, but instead I turned and crouched down, running along to the back of the house.

Chapter Eleven

When I got back into the house I could hear Harris on the stairs. "Up you go, now," he shouted, and a few seconds later I heard the trap door to the attic shut with a bang. I hid in the kitchen and waited, looking for something that would take him by surprise, something I could stab him with, but the drawers were all empty. I could feel the heat from the kitchen and I saw him come by and light a cigarette on the way out.

"Tossers," he said and walked past me to the back door. I had to decide if it was worth spending time on him, because I didn't have much left of it. It was either Harris or my friends, and I wasn't about to let them die in the attic.

I tore as fast as I could through the flames in the living room, grateful to have hiking boots on, and then rushed up the stairs. I had to jump up and stand up on the end of the banister to reach the tab hanging from the ceiling. I hoped I'd be strong enough to pull the stairs down and get the others

The Gangster's Fortune

out of the attic. I stretched up and grabbed the rope that was attached to the metal ring in the ceiling and yanked it as hard as I could. It was enough. The door in the ceiling opened and I jumped up to grab hold of the end of the stairs, hoping I'd be strong enough to pull them down. I yelled up through the hole above my head.

"Hello?"

I looked up and saw Hugh peering down at me. "You're not burned are you, Mabel?"

"I'm fine but it's getting hot. Bring the fur coat down and you can use it to get out. How's Barnaby?" I felt afraid to hear the answer.

"He's still breathing but I don't know for how much longer."

Hugh emerged with Barnaby on his shoulder and Tabby following close behind.

"Thank God you came back," Tabby said. "I thought we were done for."

"We've got to go, now," I said, "Hugh, can you manage to help Barnaby? You need to go first so you can get him out of here."

The Gangster's Fortune

"We'll see you outside," Hugh said. "Make sure you crawl along the floor. The smoke is terrible already." He pulled up his shirt to cover his mouth and picked Barnaby up, and then ran down the stairs as fast as he could. Some of the stairs gave way and the railing, which had gone up in flames, fell down into the living room.

"I'm going to have to jump the last few. Mabel, you won't be able to come down this way," Hugh shouted up the stairs to us.

"What are we going to do then?" Tabby asked, looking down the stairs. "How are we supposed to get out?"

"Let's go back up into the attic. There was a window at the far side, wasn't there? Maybe we can break it and crawl out on to the branch of a tree. It's worth trying. I don't think we can get out through the house now."

"I'm game if you are," Tabby said.

"We held hands, climbed the stairs back up into the attic and crawled along the beams to the window.

The Gangster's Fortune

"I'll kick the glass out," I said. The opening was big enough for me to crawl through but I wasn't sure if Tabby could get out this way too.

"It's not big enough for me, Mabel," she said, "and the smoke's coming up now, we don't have much time. We've had a good run for it, but I think this is goodbye." She wrapped her arms around me. "I never imagined it would end like this. I thought we'd go on forever, just finding treasure. It was so much fun."

"I'm not ready to give up yet," I said. "I won't lose you. Either we go together or not at all." I ran to the other window on the far wall and looked out. All I could see were flames shooting out from below.

"Grab the trunk," I said. "We're going to ram a hole through the wall. The ceiling in here's been leaking for years, and it's made everything rotten, including the walls. We have to try at least. That's what they used to do in the Middle Ages when they were trying to bring the drawbridge down in front of a castle. They'd ram it."

"It's nonsense, Mabel. We're not in the Middle Ages, we're stuck in a farmhouse in America and we're going to die here." She sunk down to her knees and started crying.

"I'm asking you to do one thing Tabby, just one thing." I put my hands on her shoulders. She looked up at me. "Just try. Pick it up, the trunk, bring it over to the window with me and we'll swing it against the wall."

We each picked up one end of the trunk and swung it against the wall. The trunk bounced off.

"See, it's no good," Tabby said.

"Let's try it the other way," I said, coughing because the smoke was making it hard to see. "We'll just hurl it at the wall, both at the same end and crash it through. Give it your best effort, Tabby, you're miles stronger than me. Do it as though your life depended on it."

"It does." She began coughing too.

"We'll only have one or two chances before the smoke burns our lungs and we collapse."

The Gangster's Fortune

Tabby picked up the end of the trunk and I stood beside her and we pushed as hard as we could.

"Remember that fellow in Scotland, he threw a log in the air?"

The trunk went smashing into the wall and made a dent in it.

"Again," I shouted, "and pull your t-shirt up to cover your mouth."

We rammed the wall three or four more times with the trunk until we'd created an opening under the window big enough to get Tabby through.

"Hooray," I said, "and not a moment to lose. There's a tree here we can climb out on to." I stepped out on to the roof and felt it hot under my feet. I jumped for the tree limb and swung on it until I could get my feet up to wrap around the branch further down.

"Big jump, Tabby and you're there." I watched her step in a great stride off the roof and jump for the branch a few feet from the side of the house. She swung her feet up and together we edged down the tree to the ground. We ran to the front expecting to find Hugh, Barnaby and Jules waiting for us. Instead, there were police cars. Benny was still lying unconscious beside the car, but there was no sign of either Hugh or Barnaby.

"What do you mean, they're not here?" Tabby asked Jules.

"Are they still inside?" I went over to a fireman who was spraying the flames in front of the house. "We just got out through the attic but our friends are still inside, we think." I thought of Harris and what he might have done to them.

The fireman took his axe and went to the porch, and began to knock down the door. Three more firemen went in after him. Were they both dead? They couldn't be. Policemen kept us back from the fire or I would have followed the men in. Tabby crouched on the grass, crying with Jules, who was patting her hair and telling her it was going to be ok.

I couldn't be told to do nothing, not if it meant that the boys might die, so I grabbed one of the firemen's jackets from the fire engine, one I assumed to be an extra, and a hat with an oxygen

The Gangster's Fortune

tank. I went around the back and found gloves in the pocket of the jacket. I looked for a spare oxygen tank, found one and lifted it up to see if it was full. I turned the oxygen on, twisting a dial, put the mask over my mouth and inhaled, then swung the oxygen tank on to my back.

Flames were pouring out of the back door, and the steps were completely burned up. I grabbed some boards from behind the shed that we'd seen on the way in, and piled them up so I could climb up them to the back door, not knowing if I'd fall through the porch and get trapped underneath it.

I made it through the door, and inside I saw Hugh lying on the floor and Barnaby beside him. There was a beam on Barnaby's back and it looked as though Hugh had been trying to lift it off when another beam had come down and hit Barnaby across his head.

I tried to clear the way to get them out. First I grabbed Hugh's hand and dragged him towards the door, his back on the floor. Then I pulled him down the boards, heaved him over to the grass behind the house, and rolled him over on to his side.

"Please be all right." I took my mask off and kissed him. His eyes fluttered open and he said my name, barely able to open his eyes, before he started coughing.

"Stay here and don't move a muscle, Hugh McGinley," I said, wanting to stay with him but knowing I had to do everything I could to rescue Barnaby as well.

I ran back into the house. Even more beams were coming down. I could see the firemen coming through the front door and making their way to Barnaby, who was lying in the middle of what had once been the living room. It was so hot that it felt as if my coat might melt down, on to my skin. As the front of the house completely engulfed in flames, I pointed to the back door, and one of the firemen picked Barnaby up and carried him outside.

Hugh sat up. His face was covered in black soot and he looked like he'd been through the wars. He was crying. "I thought I'd got him, but then the beams started coming down and when I tried to get

The Gangster's Fortune

him out from underneath, one fell on top of me. Luckily for me I was wearing the coat. I think it saved me. How did you get out, Mabel? How did you manage that?"

"Through the attic. There's a window up there and a branch close by, but Tabby couldn't get out of the window and so we used the trunk upstairs to ram a hole in the wall. It was so badly rotted, the wall that is, that it only took us a couple of throws to drive a hole through the wall under the window that was wide enough for us to get through."

"We need to see if Barnaby's all right. Are you strong enough to walk?"

Hugh took the fur coat off and I could see that the beam had burned right through it, almost down to his skin. When we went round to the front of the house we saw Barnaby being carried over to an ambulance. He still looked unconscious and had horrible burns on his head.

"I think we have a brain bleed," I heard someone yell.

Jules was waiting there for us with the police. She came over and hugged us. "Cliff came out and

The Gangster's Fortune

I told him to call the police; they came with the fire trucks just a few minutes ago. I'm so glad you're ok, Mabel."

Barnaby was lifted into the ambulance and driven away to the nearest hospital. As only family members could accompany a patient in an ambulance, Tabby went with him, while the rest of us watched in a daze as the ambulance pulled away, its sirens screeching.

Then the police turned to us and began questioning, asking how the fire had started.

"It was my dad, he was trying to kill my friends," I told them.

"How many of them?"

"There are four of us," I said.

"But why would someone do that," he asked, "especially your father?"

"Because my birth mother is the head of a gang and she's jealous of everyone in my life, so she sent my birth father here to kill them and take the treasure, and then take me back with him, I think."

"Take you where?" the policeman asked.

The Gangster's Fortune

"Back to England. They want me to join their gang and steal the treasure." I was so tired and exasperated I could barely speak.

"What kind of treasure are you talking about?"

"I think we found Dutch Schultz's treasure," I said. "But none of that matters right now. What we need is to go to our friend and be with him."

"How do you know it's Dutch Schultz's?"

I wanted to scream that we'd tell them everything later, but that might end up with me being arrested, so I took a deep breath and answered as calmly as I could.

"Because he had a family that lived in this house and he buried it behind the house. It ought to be in the boot of the car, unless my father stole that too. Benny tried to make off with it."

"Who's Benny?" the policeman asked. He was writing on his notepad as fast as he could and didn't look much older than us.

"That lump beside the car. We knocked him out with a shovel. He might have the keys in his pocket."

The Gangster's Fortune

"You stay here," the officer said, and walked over to Benny. He found the keys and then went to the car and opened the boot: the suitcases were inside.

"Why don't you open them?" I said. "We don't know for certain that my father didn't steal what was in them and then leave the empty cases behind." I couldn't imagine where Harris might be, even though the police and fire engines would have made him scarce, but it probably wasn't very far.

"Looks like everything's in here, gold, money, jewels. You really think this is Dutch Schultz's treasure?"

"Someone needs to find my birth father. He's got to be around here somewhere. Don't you have records you can check? You can't underestimate him."

"No one saw the man you're describing." The officer said, looking like he thought we'd set the fire ourselves.

I wanted to shout at him that he had to believe us, that we were telling the truth, and he needed to start searching immediately, and stop asking questions that could all be answered later. But instead I said, "He must have found another way out, through the back forest."

Where was he? I looked about frantically, wondering if he might appear and just start firing off rounds of ammunition. He had disappeared and the policeman took his information and ours and told us we could go. Then he loaded Benny into the back of the police car for further questioning.

"You have to find Harris Walker," I told them as we walked towards Jules' car, knowing that somehow he'd managed to slip away again and that no one could do anything about it. When the three of us were alone in the car we just sat there, feeling stunned.

"What just happened?" Jules said.

"The end, that's what happened. My birth father tried to burn all my friends to death. It's over. They win. I'll go with them if they leave you all alone. We can't do this anymore, Jules. I'm the one to blame. You both know it's true."

"What are you going to do, Mabel?" Jules asked.

"I have to go home and start all over again."

"I'm not giving you up, Mabel, not again," Hugh said.

"I'm sorry, but you haven't got any choice."

"Don't say that," Hugh said.

"I have to."

Jules drove Hugh and me to the hospital and when we pulled up I was so frightened I could hardly dare go inside. Hugh held my hand and Jules put her arm around my neck. How had it all come to this? In a hospital again, with one of my friends in grave danger.

The Gangster's Fortune

Chapter Twelve

We were sitting in the waiting room when Tabby came back in. She walked over to us, sobbing. "He stopped breathing in the ambulance. Barnaby's gone. He's dead. He's dead."

"What?" I asked, scarcely believing it was true.

"His brain. One of the beams hit him so hard on the head that it killed him. They say he was dead before they even brought him out of the house."

"Tabby, Tabby," I moaned, trying to catch my breath.

"It was an accident, Mabel," Hugh said. "It could have been any one of us."

"But they came for me. They wanted to get you all out of the picture but now Barnaby's no longer with us and it's all my fault. I did this, and now I need to find my own way to stop her. Jules, can you take me to the airport, please?" I asked.

The Gangster's Fortune

"You can't just walk away like this, Mabel," Tabby said. "It's not right. So, please, stay with us. Say your farewell to Barnaby. You can go in, they said you could."

She was right. I couldn't just walk out. I had to see him with my own eyes.

"All right," I said. "Yes, you're right. I do need to say goodbye."

Tabby took me by the hand and led me down the hallway to the room he was in. I stepped over to the bed he was lying on. His face looked peaceful. There was a little smile on his lips but nothing more. It looked as if he might wake up at any moment. Then I saw how awfully the fire had burned him. I kissed his forehead and held him in my arms. I couldn't believe he was gone and I wanted him back.

I couldn't imagine how hard this had to be for Tabby. She was going to hate me forever. Maybe not now but later, she would blame me for this.

"I'm so sorry this happened to you, Barnaby," I said. I laid my head on his chest, listening for a heartbeat, but his chest was empty of any sound. I wanted to thump his chest, to restart his heart, but instead I just put my head on it and started sobbing.

"It's all my fault. You never should have been in that house, none of you should have come with me. I'm so sorry."

Tabby sat down on a chair beside the bed. She put her head on her knees and started to sob.

"I'm going to make this right," I said to Barnaby, closing his eyes. "I'm going to make this right."

A nurse came in and said she wanted to put a sheet over his face.

Tabby wouldn't let her. "Not yet, we're not ready for that yet." We both held his hands and took turns talking softly to him.

"I'm so sorry, Tabby."

"I know you are."

I felt the weight of the world on my shoulders. "I need to go," I said.

"What is it that can't wait, Mabel?" she asked.

"It's time I stopped putting you in harm's way. I have to go home. I don't think you'll be hearing from me again."

"But you can't just leave, Mabel. Harris has gone now. We need you here with us to bring Barnaby home. Please say you will. I don't want to lose you both on the same day. That would be just too cruel."

"Sorry," I murmured. "Don't know what I was thinking." I had just had a vision of Harris marching into the hospital ward and gunning down the rest of them, but that didn't bear mentioning now.

"What's the matter, Mabel?"

"I'm just so scared he's going to come in here and finish the job."

"They said they're going to post officers outside the door and we'll be under police protection until we get home," Tabby said.

"They did?"

"Yes, Mabel. He's not going to hurt us anymore. You were right not to want to come and we should have listened to you; and now Barnaby's dead, my perfect, beautiful brother. He loved you, you know. He told me so, and I didn't really believe him. I thought he just had a crush on you and it would pass. The more he got to know you... I can't explain it, it's certainly never happened to me."

I looked over at Barnaby. I couldn't believe that we were sitting in a hospital room just talking, with him there, dead, right beside us. It felt normal, as if his eyes would suddenly flutter open and then he'd cough and we'd tell him that he'd been out cold for longer than we'd liked, but now he was back with us. And I started to weep again.

"And Mabel, you have to understand that what he wanted, more than anything, was to come and see New York, and go on an adventure. And yes, he was scared and he didn't like the guns, but he wanted to be here so he could protect you."

"And all he got in return for that was dying. I gave him that."

Tabby took my hand. How could she be so forgiving?

"He had the time of his life," she went on. "I can't believe he's gone, though. I thought, well, I never thought it would be like this, so fast, in a matter of hours. I never had a chance to say goodbye to him, I mean I did in the ambulance but he wasn't really awake any more. He was already gone and I'm just so sad. Do you think his spirit is still in this room? Do you think he's watching us? He'd hate to see us so sad, crying like this. But I feel he's here. Not that far after all. I can't explain it but I can feel him."

"I'll get us some tea," I said, because I needed a moment to go to the loo and just bawl my eyes out.

"No, Mabel, don't leave us, please. Don't leave me." She pulled the blankets up to just under Barnaby's neck and laid her head back on his chest. "He was always so kind to me. You know, he always watched out for me, played games with me on weekends. He didn't have to but we loved each other's company. He talked to me about things in a way my parents couldn't and nothing was ever too much trouble for him. And for years, Mabel, years, he asked me about you, about what you were like, and after we found the paintings he said he'd wished he'd been there to find them too. He was a treasure hunter in his heart. Weren't you, my dear brother?"

The Gangster's Fortune

"I need some tea," I said, tears streaming down my face.

Tabby didn't seem to hear me. "He liked you so much, Mabel, never liked any other girls that way. I think they just bored him to tears. He could have had anyone, but he wanted you." She looked at me.

"I'm so sorry, Tabby, I liked him so much. At first, I couldn't believe it either."

Tabby's hands were shaking.

"Come on, let's go and see the others," I said.

"I can't, I can't leave him yet."

"Well, I'll go on my own then." I walked around to her side of the bed, looking at her with her brother, gave her shoulder a squeeze and patted her hair.

"It's never going to be the same again, is it, Mabel?"

"No, it's not. But I really think he's here with us, I can feel him just sort of hovering too."

There was a knock at the door and Hugh came in. "Shall I get you some tea?" he asked.

We nodded and I stayed by Tabby's side.

A few minutes later he came back in. "It's America, they've only got coffee here."

"That's fine," Tabby said, not really hearing him.

"Where's Jules?" I asked.

"Calling her mum, and the police have come back to question us."

"Hugh," I said. "What are we going to say?"

"We'll tell the truth, of course. That we found Dutch Schultz's treasure and if someone still has the diary after the fire, we'll give them that too, and then we'll go home."

"Yes, of course," I said.

+++

When the police came to question us, hours later, Barnaby had been already taken out of the room by the hospital staff and Jules' mother Vivian had come to drive us back to the city, we thought. But Vivian wouldn't speak to us directly. She just stood there with her back to us, or went outside to smoke.

"My mom says I need to go home with her," Jules said. "She came with George and he's going to bring you to the airport."

"I'm not going anywhere," Tabby said. "I need to take Barnaby home, so I'll have to wait for my parents to arrive."

Jules went outside to talk to her mother, and then came back in again. "She says you can't stay with us. She's afraid something might happen to me. I'm sorry."

"If you could bring our things here from the cottage, we can find a hotel room, can't we?" I suggested.

"She's already advised George to do that," Jules said. "I have to go. She is so much more heartless than I could ever have imagined. So it's goodbye, then. I'm sorry I can't help but I'll write and we'll keep in touch and I'll come over and see you. We're all almost adults. They can't keep us apart if we want to be together." She hugged each of us and told us she loved us and that she'd always want to stay in touch and then she left.

"So that's how it ends with Jules," Hugh said.

Soon after, more policemen came but I didn't recognize the one I'd been talking to outside the house.

"Did you find Harris Walker?" I asked them.

They were sitting on the chairs beside us in the waiting room, taking our names and asking where Jules was and if they could question her too.

"Her mother came to take her home. She didn't think it was safe for us to stay with her," Hugh said.

"She does have a point," one of the policeman said, looking at me, "if this Harris tried to burn you all to death, all except you. You're Mabel, right?"

This policeman was older, with a fat tummy and a great big double chin. "You know people have been looking for this treasure for years," he went on. "The papers will want to talk to you."

"Have you managed to contact my father yet?" I asked, not caring about the papers or

The Gangster's Fortune

anything else. "He's a police officer in England." I gave them his card.

"We'll be putting you all up in a hotel for a few nights until one of your parents comes to claim your brother." He looked over at Tabby. "I'm so sorry. It's a young age to lose a sibling." He cleared his throat and rubbed his forehead, taking off his black hat with its shiny rim. "We have confirmed that the treasure you found is that of Dutch Schultz and we have also learned that he had a daughter named Desdemona. We will be contacting her once we determine if she is still alive."

"Sorry, that's something we don't know," Tabby said, taking the diary out of her bag. "Somehow it survived the fire, but my brother didn't." She handed it to the officers.

"The treasure is estimated to be worth at least $7 million."

"What will you do with it?" Tabby asked.

"I expect we'll know the answer to that question when we find your Miss Desdemona. The government will take its chunk but they can't take it all."

The Gangster's Fortune

+++

Weeks later, when we'd finally made it back to England, they held Barnaby's funeral. I kept in the distance, watching Tabby and Hugh. As his coffin was being lowered into the ground I wondered if someone might charge over and tell me to leave, but no one did. We'd all had a terrible shock. I hadn't spoken to either of them since coming home. I thought they were well rid of me.

Not wanting to cause a stir, I wanted to be among the first to leave, but before I managed to do so, I saw a man and woman making their way over towards where I was standing, apart from the group. The woman looked as if she was in her sixties. Her skin was the colour of light chocolate and her hair was swept up and covered with a small hat and veil. She was dressed all in black, wearing a fine black jacket and skirt and small heels.

The Gangster's Fortune

"Mabel Hartley?" she asked, as she approached me. "I'm Desdemona Early Covington."

I stared at her, speechless, and then she reached out her hand and I took it, uncertain what to say, what to do next.

"I came here to pay my respects. I understand this young man Barnaby was a friend of yours, and he died soon after finding Dutch Schultz's treasure."

"Yes, that's right. When we talked to the police, they weren't sure if you could be found. I imagine some of the treasure will be yours now?"

"It's a little soon for that, might you walk me back to my car? This is my friend, Patrick, he's a colleague of mine, with New York University. I'm a professor at the University of California, Berkeley. You may have heard of it."

"You're a professor now?" I smiled at her. "Perhaps you know that we found your diary from when you were a little girl, and it sounded like you had a really hard time losing both your parents at such a young age. I'm sorry for that."

The Gangster's Fortune

"That was a long time ago. Now I teach courses in American history."

We walked together past the funeral vehicles and then a long line of cars with a bench behind them.

"What has life been like for you?" I asked her. "Especially knowing your father was..." I didn't know what to say and I didn't want to offend her.

"Knowing he was Dutch Schultz? It was a relief to know he was dead."

I could sympathize with that.

"He was kind to me when I was a child, and oh, how I loved him and my momma too, but back then black and white folks didn't mix. So, *I* was a secret."

I knew all about secrets: nothing good ever came from them.

"I don't want to bore you," she said, putting her hand on mine, "but I feel you might understand, given the violence that killed your friend in Phoenicia."

"Please go on," I implored her, placing my other hand on hers.

The Gangster's Fortune

"As I grew up, I always wondered why I never had the same rights and privileges as white folk. We were second-class citizens, sometimes treated worse than that. We weren't allowed to mix with white folks. Then things began to change, slowly, and people began to think differently. They began to think we might be equals, as you and I are, Mabel. And something changed in me, I began to see education as a way to learn about who I really was inside. And once I caught the bug, it never let up and I just kept writing and teaching and learning myself, you see, about what might be in my future."

"I like learning too," I said. "I like finding things that have been lost and understanding how people lived the way they did, and that is something I don't think I'll ever lose. But now I have to give that all up."

"Why ever would you do that, child?"

"Because it's the only way. It seems you've found peace in your life and that's what I want too. I want my friends and family to be free and out of danger, and until I change things will never be right. My father's waiting for me, and so is my birth mother. They're both in criminal worlds, just as Dutch was, and they threaten to take everything away from me that I hold dear."

"They can't take those parts of you that you don't give away to them. You keep those parts close. The parts that make you feel love and friendship and the parts that make you such a great treasure hunter. I wanted to thank you personally, Mabel, for finding my father's treasure. I imagine some of it will come to me and if it does, I've decided I'd like to give back. I'd like to give scholarships to young women of color, who see more for themselves in the world, young women who have your spirit and passion for learning about the world and what they might bring to it. So, I'll be setting that up, all in good time. We women can change the world, you know."

"That seems like a good thing to do, Miss Covington."

"Please, call me Dessie." She took my hand and reached forward to whisper something in my ear. I bent forward and listened, believing that one day I might be free too.

The Gangster's Fortune

"You're made for much more than this, Mabel Hartley. You come see me when you have things settled and I'll be waiting for you at my door." She passed me her card with her information, and I took it.

"Thanks, Dessie. "

We looked at each other, our eyes warming second by second, until our arms wrapped about each other in a gentle hug.

"Your friends there seem like they're waiting on you."

"I know, but I can't."

"Something pressing on your mind, child?"

"Yes, there is."

"I'll be seeing you then, Mabel. Take care."

I shook her hand and then walked away from the cemetery, knowing I may never see any of my friends again, and that it was my choice.

My father was waiting in the car on the ridge of the hill. "Time to get to work then?" he said as I got in. I knew we were headed to London's MI5 headquarters by Vauxhall Bridge, over the River Thames.

The Gangster's Fortune

Working with others by joining the intelligence community was the only way to stop my mother for good. I would be trained in intelligence with munitions, martial arts, weaponry and technology. I couldn't wait to get started but it meant leaving everything and everyone I cared about behind. I felt sad and wondered how long it would take to track her down and join her ranks.

Grace was free now: they'd let her out of prison just after I'd arrived home. All the witnesses had recanted their testimony. All the more reason to protect my friends. It felt like a last resort, but there was no other way.

Once I became a trusted member of Grace's operation, only then could I start to take her apart, bit by bit. Part of me knew that learning the circumstances around my birth and truly understanding her obsession with me would be her undoing. I hoped I was right. It was the only way to keep Tabby and Hugh safe and I wasn't prepared to endanger them ever again. My heart broke, thinking of not having them in my life, but after what

The Gangster's Fortune

had happened to Barnaby, it was the only way forward. The only way to truly stop a monster.

I felt for the locket around my neck that Hugh had given me in Scotland. Inside, I'd added a photo of Tabby along with the picture of Hugh and me. I knew I was fighting for their freedom, their futures and our friendship, if I could make it back alive.

Author Biography

Jane Reddington is truly Mabel Hartley's biggest fan. After working on the series for more than 10 years, Mabel continues to inspire Jane to write, research and travel with Mabel on her adventures.

Never has Jane had more fun writing, and sharing her books than in 2017. *The Gangster's Fortune* is Jane's favorite book in the series because it takes the treasure hunters to New York City, one of Jane's favorite places.

Look out for *Mabel Hartley and the Vigilante's Secret,* the fifth and final book in 2018 where Mabel learns the secrets to her mother's obsession and how she can defeat the monster that threatens to destroy everything Mabel holds dear.

Visit www.janereddington.com to find out more about Mabel Hartley and her adventures.

Made in the USA
Columbia, SC
06 April 2018